Broken Mind

Oliver Rixon

Broken Mind

Oliver Rixon

HollyBlue Publishing

First published in Great Britain in 2014

Holly Blue Publishing
www.hollybluepublishing.co.uk

Copyright © Oliver Rixon 2014

All rights reserved. No part of this book may be reproduced or transmitted in any form or by any means, electronic or mechanical, including photocopying, recording or by any information storage and retrieval systems, without permission in writing from the publisher.

The author and publisher have made every effort to ensure that the external website and email addresses included in this book are correct and up to date at the time of going to press. The author and publisher are not responsible for the content, quality or continuing accessibility of the sites.

ISBN-10: 150311077X
ISBN-13: 978-1503110779

A sequel to
Broken Mirror

Contents

Chapter One: a taste for murder 8

Chapter two: bad news 24

Chapter three: revelations 40

Chapter four: family 58

Chapter five: a deadly secret 76

Chapter six: tempers rising 86

Chapter seven: a crisis of conscience 98

Chapter eight: ghosts of the past 108

Chapter nine: broken mind 122

Chapter ten: betrayal 128

Chapter eleven: regrets 140

Chapter eighteen: a bargain with God 220

Chapter twenty: retribution 232

Chapter One: a taste for murder

Seven years on…

Reverend Lucas Wheelan had his fist tight around the young man's scrawny neck. He was squeezing so hard the man's eyes were bulging and bloodshot. The wretched youth was obviously terrified. He stared pleadingly at the minister as his life slowly ebbed away. His face and neck were congested and rapidly turning a ghastly shade of puce. Wheelan could feel the man's windpipe crunching beneath his fingers as his neck muscles gave way to the inevitability of death.

Wheelan grinned salaciously. He was enjoying this…

'Nobody steels from me', Wheelan rasped through gritted teeth, the effort of throttling what he considered to be a low life druggie was beginning to take its toll. It was taking all his strength to keep up the pressure on the emaciated throat of his victim and his hand was beginning to ache.

Wheelan had his knee in the man's puny chest. He was pushing him against the gravestone below. The Reverend was fending off his victim's weakening struggles with his other hand. 'Die, you bastard', he said. No one will miss the likes of you.

The old scar running down Wheelan's cheek began to itch. The ugly gash was a remnant from a past that he'd rather forget.

Wheelan shoved his knee harder into the man's chest.

As the ache in his hand intensified, he briefly released his grip. The man coughed and drew a laboured, rasping breath before Wheelan slammed his forearm into the man's throat, leaning in and using his body weight to increase the pressure and sever his lifeline.

The youth's throat was trapped between the solid limestone of the grave and the crushing pressure of Wheelan's weight. He felt the cartilage of the man's windpipe crunch and give way beneath his arm.

The youth was weakening as he tried to mouth words that couldn't form – his last breath trapped inside his lungs.

Wheelan watched as his victim lost consciousness. His body slumped as all resistance finally ceased. His eyes became empty and lifeless, gazing unseeingly into the distance.

Satisfied with his work, the minister released the pressure on his windpipe. The man was dead. The mark of his forearm was heavily indented into his throat and there were deep contusions on his neck from the struggle. His head slumped back and to one side, blood-stained secretions dribbling from his mouth.

Wheelan stood and leered over the dead man. He felt a dark satisfaction that he hadn't experienced in a long time. His knew life had been a travesty, marked only by hypocrisy and his spineless lack of integrity. He'd felt weak and tortured much of the time but in this moment, he was in complete control – he felt liberated.

Wheelan straightened up, taking a deep breath. He adjusted his jacket and rubbed the ache away from his hand and forearm.

His angry rage was morphing into malicious gratification.

He was revelling in the feeling of power he had from killing another human being. It felt uplifting and thoroughly intoxicating. In the moment, he had no conscience whatsoever about what he was doing – he simply became immersed in the experience of taking the life of another.

Wheelan looked up, suddenly aware that he was out in the open and exposed. He glanced around but could see no one – it was still early in the morning. The beach ahead and the slipway to the road were deserted. The tide was full in and crashing on the pebbles less than one hundred yards away. Wheelan took a deep breath of salt air. The dead man lay slumped and dishevelled over the ancient gravestone at the side of the chapel. The concrete slab that covered the grave had been shifted marginally to reveal the open space inside. The youth had tried to steel Wheelan's stash of cocaine, but was caught in the act.

He knew the young man slightly – he'd recently started buying drugs from Wheelan but he obviously couldn't be trusted. He had the audacity to steel from him in broad daylight. He probably thought the chapel was deserted. Well it was much of the time these days. He was young and stupid, Wheelan thought, but now he was dead. The minister wasn't going to risk his nice little side-line business for a desperate and unpredictable drug addict. Wheelan made a mental note to move his stash somewhere safer and to be more careful about whom he sold to. He had plenty of regulars he could trust – it wasn't worth the trouble of dealing with scum like him, he thought.

Wheelan knew he had to dispose of the body but Mary, his housekeeper, was due soon – he'd just have to move it out of sight and bury him after dark.

Wheelan grabbed the youth by the wrists. The body thudded onto the ground as he pulled him off the grave, his head hanging limply to one side. The man's clothing rode up to reveal his pale emaciated torso, as Wheelan dragged him backward toward the back of the chapel. He was covered with grotesque tattoos and scars. The minister hauled him unceremoniously up the short gravel path into a windowless store room at the rear of the chapel. He dumped his malnourished body into a corner and covered it with an old tarpaulin.

Wheelan caught his breath, brushed the dust from his hands and closed the door of the room, the damp swollen wood catching on the uneven stone floor. He slammed it firmly shut.

Wheelan then went back to re-seal the grave, first checking the plastic packages inside were intact. His modest stash of cocaine was undamaged – he'd caught the thief in time. The old stone slab was engraved, '*Here lies Thomas Davies, beloved husband, father and grandfather. He died of pneumonia, 1787*'. The words were weathered and worn - barely perceptible now. Wheelan kicked some loosened stones back onto the narrow path and quickly checked for the tell-tale signs of a struggle.

It was all clear.

Checking yet again for potential witnesses, Wheelan strode back to the manse, just inland of the chapel. He took a deep breath and ran his gnarled fingers through his hair. At seventy, he still had a thick head of hair, now liberally peppered with grey. He was reasonably fit, considering his unhealthy lifestyle.

Wheelan's hand was trembling slightly as the adrenaline rush began to wear off. His stomach was cramping into a painful knot.

Crunching over the loose stones of the driveway, he reached the manse. Hanging his jacket on a hook already bulging with coats, he headed for the sink in the cluttered kitchen to wash his hands. The minister wanted to rid himself of the filthy stench from that light-fingered bastard; to cleanse himself of the murder he'd just committed. His fiery temper was cooling...

Wheelan scrubbed furiously at his hands, his mind becoming numb. He had just strangled someone to death, but after the heady rush of anger, the realisation was only just starting to kick in. What the hell had prompted him to react so violently? He'd dealt with what he considered to be the dregs of humanity like him plenty of times and sometimes wished them dead but this – this was an unexpectedly strong reaction on his part. What had happened to the reformed character he'd become over the past few years?

His thoughts were interrupted by a door slamming shut in the hallway and Mary's voice calling out, 'Lucas! Are you there?'

Wheelan winced at the shrill pitch of Mary's voice – and what about a bit of respect? She used to call me 'Reverend', he thought.

Mary Jones bustled into the kitchen, carrying bags of groceries. She plonked them down on the table and slipped off her overcoat, throwing it over the back of a chair. She leaned over and kissed Wheelan's cheek, grabbing him by firmly the arm as he tried to wipe his hands on a towel.

'It's getting chilly out there now', she said lightly, referring to the first signs of Autumn and the sea breeze that was strengthening by the day.

As Mary busied herself with putting the groceries away, Wheelan wiped the sticky lipstick from his cheek with the damp towel, leaving a bright red stain. He wished she wouldn't do that. She was getting far too familiar, he thought. He'd have to put a stop to it. She was beginning to assume they would be more than just friends, when he'd never given her the slightest encouragement.

Wheelan's hands were still trembling from the encounter with the youth he'd just throttled – the youth that still lay slumped in his store room. His mind started descending into anxious thoughts about getting caught when he stopped himself abruptly. No-one cares a damn about a thieving lout like that, he silently reasoned. His mother's probably drugged up to her eyeballs and would be glad to see the back of him anyway. She'll only notice he's missing when her heroine runs out. The kid was involved with a bad crowd and any one of them would have stabbed him without a second thought. The world was well rid of him – why should he care.

Mary began her usual tirade of meaningless chit-chat and Wheelan dragged up a kitchen chair, sitting down at the antique pine table. He had resigned himself to the next thirty minutes of her persistent gossip about the people of the village. It was a distraction, at least, while he came to terms with the fact that he'd just killed someone with his bare hands.

As Mary's voice droned on in the background, Wheelan felt empty. Many of the people she talked about had been his parishioners and, he'd hoped, his lifeline to a more normal life after Terry Morgan's fatal car crash. Chance had finally freed him from Morgan's relentless blackmail but he'd failed to find any lasting happiness. The people he'd hoped would be his salvation turned out to be as hypocritical as him in many ways – they could be self-absorbed and insensitive, despite outward appearances to the contrary, and they were constantly bitching about each other and complaining. The people he had turned to were shallow and soulless just as he'd always suspected – there was little true friendship there. Finally he'd settled for a life alone and had to admit he was better off without people most of the time.

Now he had to contend with Mary. She was getting ahead of herself. What made her think he would ever entertain the idea of them as a couple? He looked up and she smiled at him flirtatiously, her chubby cheeks bulging, turning her bright eyes into narrow slits. He frowned back at her. Why the bloody hell didn't she get the message, he thought. Yes they'd been friends for a long time but that didn't give her carte blanche to assume there would ever be more. He couldn't bring himself to use the word 'lovers' – he shuddered at the thought. Even his days of taking prostitutes into his bed were over. Mary didn't have a hope in hell.

Mary placed a mug of tea in front of him and a hefty wedge of her home-made chocolate cake, complete with dark chocolate trimmings. Now that's more like it, he thought. All I want from you is your housekeeping skills and your cooking – that's what I pay you for. You can forget the rest. He broke off a piece of the cake – it was sweet and melting deliciously in his mouth. It suddenly struck him as surreal to be eating cake and chatting as if nothing had happened when there was a corpse in his store room just yards away.

Wheelan shrugged off the thought, distracting himself with the cake and tea. His fingers were still trembling slightly as he drew the mug to his lips. As he swallowed the hot liquid, a searing pain shot through his chest and into his stomach. He'd been plagued with indigestion and heartburn for months. Wheelan stopped eating and pushed the rest of the cake away from him. It was agonizing on times.

'What's the matter, Lucas?' Mary had seen him wincing with pain.

Wheelan shook his head unable to speak for a few seconds. 'I'm ok – just heartburn.'

'Not my cooking, I hope.' Mary said, jovially.

'No, I get it with everything I eat lately – I forgot my tablets this morning.' Wheelan stood up and reached for his anti-reflux medication in the kitchen drawer. That wretched drug addict thief had distracted him from his usual routine. He threw his head back as he downed the tablet with a swig of milk from the bottle.

'You should see a doctor.' Mary said in a stern yet motherly tone.

Wheelan waved away the suggestion, 'I'm alright – stop fussing.' He rarely visited the doctor and wasn't about to for a bout of indigestion.

Mary scowled at him as she continued putting the groceries away.

Wheelan ignored her and sat down to finish his mug of tea, the rest of the cake left uneaten.

Mary put some tinned food into the cupboard and quietly stepped behind him, bending to put her arms around him. 'You know I care about you, Lucas', she said, turning her head to kiss his cheek once again.

Wheelan's tolerance snapped. 'Stop that' – he spat the words as he slammed his mug down on the table and shrugged her away.

Mary pulled back, startled.

Wheelan was irritated and in pain. He hated being smothered and he knew the time had come to confront Mary about her growing but unwanted affection for him. Wheelan was silent for several awkward seconds before he spoke.

'Mary, you have to stop this'. He tried to calm his voice, not wishing really wishing to hurt her feelings.

'Stop what?' she asked.

'This... this being affectionate with me. You seem to be getting the wrong idea.' He avoided looking at her.

'What do you mean – the wrong idea? The wrong idea about what?'

Mary sounded hurt but Wheelan knew he had to continue. 'You're assuming I want us to be more than just friends but I don't want that. There's not going to be a relationship between us. Not now or ever. You have to realise that.'

Mary could only manage a shocked 'Oh'. She obviously wasn't expecting to hear that from him.

Wheelan seized his chance to put a stop to her ideas of claiming him as potential husband material once and for all. 'I know we've known each other for many years, Mary, and I'm fond of you but I just want a housekeeper and a friend – OK?' Wheelan still couldn't look at her.

Suddenly Mary grabbed his shoulder and spun him around to face her, her piercing blue eyes now boring into his, her face just inches away. 'How could you treat me like this after all we've been through? I helped you look after little Kate for all those years and I've been a loyal friend. You owe me more than this!' Mary was clearly annoyed.

'What do you mean I owe you?' Wheelan felt trapped, it was going to be harder than he'd anticipated.

'I always thought we'd be together – I thought you wanted that too'. Mary's eyes were welling up with tears and she was watching him with sadness and disappointment.

Wheelan gently pushed her hand from his shoulder and she straightened up, leaning against the kitchen counter. Her arms were folded protectively – waiting for the answer she'd been hoping for.

'Mary, I'm sorry to disappoint you. Perhaps I gave you the wrong impression but really – all I want is a housekeeper. We can be just friends can't we? Isn't that enough at our age?' Mary's tears were softening him up but he was determined to get his message across.

Mary dabbed her eyes with a tattered tissue she found in her pocket but said nothing, her emotions obviously upsetting her.

Wheelan felt awkward. He might be a sadistic killer but he did have a heart. He had to admit that Mary *had* been a loyal friend all those years. Perhaps he did owe her more...

Her tears finally got the better of him and he rose from his seat and moved toward her with a welcoming gesture. She threw her arms around him, sobbing into his shoulder. He patted her lightly on the back, not quite knowing how to react.

'I know you've been lonely since your husband died – it's been years now, I know, but you deserve better than me, Mary. Really you do'. Wheelan meant it. He was well aware of his dark brooding moods, his short temper and his lack of tolerance.

Mary sobbed quietly on his shoulder for a few moments then pulled back, drying her tears. A moment later her mood changed. 'Well, let's see how things work out. You might have a change of heart!' She looked directly at him – an unspoken question in her eyes.

Wheelan knew that was highly unlikely but decided to leave it at that for now. He couldn't cope with more of Mary's tears today. He had enough to contend with.

'I'm sorry Mary'. It was all he could manage.

She shot him a look of superiority – the look she gave him when she knew she was right. 'I know you better than you think Reverend.'

Then she was gone, the front door closing firmly behind her.

Wheelan sighed as he heard car tyres crunching on the gravel driveway as she pulled away. He could do without this from Mary. Why couldn't she accept that her feelings for him were not reciprocated? They'd managed without any sort of romantic entanglement all these years – why now did she want to cling onto him? Was she after his money? For all she knew he had the modest retirement pension of the clergy – she didn't know he had a sizeable income from his drug dealing with Terry Morgan. Even after Morgan's death, Wheelan had managed to keep his little empire going with a few regular clients. But he'd made sure he'd covered his tracks – Mary knew nothing of his sordid and secret life of crime or the modest stash of money he'd managed to accumulate.

Thinking of drugs reminded him – he had a dead body to dispose of...

Wheelan waited until it was almost dusk. He'd sat in his armchair cogitating over his relapse for most of the day. The years since Morgan's death had been relatively normal. He'd worked at his job as a minister, kept his drug dealing activities undercover and kept mostly to himself. No dramas until this damned low-life appeared this morning.

Wheelan's indigestion had thankfully eased. He finished off Mary's cake and even managed another large wedge. Mary had stormed off without making his evening meal as she usually did. He couldn't blame her, but he couldn't face cooking for himself. The cake would have to do.

Wheelan accepted the fact that he had killed again but the worst of it was that this time, he'd actually enjoyed it. Now he had to get rid of the evidence and he wasn't looking forward to it.

He thought about his options and decided against leaving the man's corpse in the cave. He'd left Helen's body there when he was young and naive but it had been nothing but trouble, with the tide breaking up her skeleton and scattering her bones where they could be found. He wouldn't make that mistake again.

Although it had been over thirty five years since he'd killed Helen, his first victim, he clearly remembered the deeply unpleasant task of disposing of the body. He'd had Morgan's help back then but now he was on his own with it. Helen's body had been crushed with the fall from the cliff and there was a lot of blood and mess to clean up but at least this would be cleaner. The youth was tall but lightweight and there was no blood this time, apart from a small dribble from his mouth. Wheelan decided to hide the body in one of the old tombs in the chapel graveyard. There hadn't been a traditional burial for many years since most families opted for cremation. The ancient graves were relatively easy to open. Thanks to soil compaction over centuries, they had a reasonable amount of space between the gravestone and the soil below and were perfect for hiding drugs, money and corpses. He knew which grave he would use – an ancient stone tomb at the side of the chapel. All he needed was a crowbar.

Wheelan went outside to check that nobody was around to witness what he was up to. The beach was generally quiet, especially at this time of day, but he had to make sure – he'd been caught out before. A strong breeze was coming in from the sea and he shivered slightly. The summer was coming to an end.

Wheelan scanned the area; the beach, the cliff tops, the slipway to the road and the woodland to the rear of the manse. Thankfully, the place was deserted – it was all clear to dispose of the body without being seen. It helped that darkness was falling, the vividness of the red sky to the west fading rapidly as the sun disappeared beneath the horizon. The tide was way down the beach, exposing a large stretch of golden sand.

Wheelan rolled his shirt sleeves up to the elbow and made his way to the chapel store room where the man's body lay. He pushed open the door and searched for a crowbar. He found it propped against the wall and used it to open one of the graves. With a few hefty shoves, the limestone lid of the tomb shifted and Wheelan peered inside. There was definitely room to squeeze in the man's puny body. He left the grave open and went back to the store room, placing the crowbar on a tool rack.

Wheelan removed the tarpaulin and spluttered as a cloud of dust filled the air. The youth's body was still slouched in a semi-sitting position against the wall; his head slumped onto his chest. The blood-stained secretions from his mouth had dried, leaving behind a dark stain streaked down his chin and clothing. Wheelan grabbed the man's wrist ready to drag him to the grave. But the body was stiff and unyielding. Several hours after death, rigor mortis had set in and the body felt icy cold to the touch. Wheelan recoiled in disgust and immediately released the wrist. But he had to dispose of the body...

His skin was crawling as he seized the man's cold clammy arm and felt the unnatural stiffness of his body as he'd tried to drag him away from the wall. It gave him the creeps and he dropped the body again.

Wheelan searched around for some gardening gloves. They were thick and at least he'd be spared from touching the corpse with his bare hands again. He shuddered at the thought. He grabbed him by the ankles this time. The body toppled over onto its side with a thud, still curled stiffly into a slouched position. He dragged it out of the room and down the path toward the earmarked grave.

It was heavy and cumbersome but Wheelan made steady progress, pulling the rigid corpse behind him with one hand. He easily covered the thirty yards to the open tomb.

Wheelan yanked the body over the stone side of the grave, shuffling it into position. It fitted – just – but the man's legs were sticking out. He would have to flatten the body in order to seal the grave.

Wheelan tried rearranging the corpse to accommodate the legs but it just wouldn't fit. The stiffness of rigor mortis had frozen the muscles and connective tissue into a semi-sitting position. There was no other option; Wheelan had to break the stiffness in the youth's legs.

He grabbed the right leg and steadying the emaciated torso with his other hand, he pushed until he felt the hip joint give way. The leg snapped straight. He held the left leg and again pushed against it, but it wouldn't give. He tried again but to no avail. The corpse lay with one stiff leg jutting out almost comically from the grave. He would have to get more leverage. Wheelan manoeuvred the body so that it lay on its side. It was facing away from him, still with the left leg stiff and sticking out. Wheelan braced against the leg with one hand and the front of the torso with the other and shoved his foot in the man's lower back. Pushing with his foot, he pulled back; the resistance finally breaking the stiffened hip joint. The leg straightened…

Wheelan was breathless from the exertion and quickly scanned the area around him once again. Still all clear, he confirmed. He finally managed to shove the body into the grave and it fitted with just centimetres to spare.

He threw the gardening gloves in on top of the fetid corpse. He couldn't imagine wanting to wear those again. Then with a few jolts, he replaced the ancient stone lid of the grave and checked for any sign of disturbance where he'd dragged the corpse down the path. In the growing gloom, he glanced around quickly once more and satisfied that the coast was clear; he made his way back to the manse, the disagreeable task complete.

The minister decided it was time for a well-deserved whiskey.

Wheelan reached the corner of the chapel and suddenly felt a wave of nausea rise up from his stomach. He stopped, clutching his abdomen as the queasy feeling intensified.

He started retching and stumbled over to the shrubs just in time to vomit into the undergrowth.

Repulsed, he re-tasted the chocolate cake but now it was mixed with an unpleasant metallic taste.

In the darkness he failed to notice the fresh blood...

Chapter two: bad news

Jenny tenderly cradled the old lady's gnarled, arthritic hand. She was dying with no family or friends left to share her final transition. Jenny had stayed with her all morning, talking to her and comforting her. She'd been reluctant to leave her side, her experience telling her that death was close.

Jenny still worked voluntarily as a nurse at the hospice in addition to her hospital work. Usually she offered a few hours every week but Ethel Smith had no one left in the world and Jenny couldn't see her spend her last moments alone. Jenny had volunteered a second day to spend with Ethel.

The old lady feebly squeezed a frail and trembling hand around Jenny's. She was mouthing words, but it was difficult to make them out. Was she trying to ask for something? Jenny stroked Ethel's fragile arm. 'Are you OK Ethel? Do you need anything?' Jenny asked.

The old lady opened her eyes briefly and turned her head to look at Jenny. 'They're here. They've come for me'. She smiled and Jenny could see the joy in her pale blue eyes.

'Who's there?' Jenny asked.

'My husband and mother; they're waiting for me'. Ethel smiled again, her delicate, paper thin skin wrinkling deeply around her eyes.

She seemed happy, Jenny thought as she returned the smile.

'My dear, they told me you would understand. That you've been to the other side'. Ethel's voice was barely a whisper.

Jenny knew what the old lady meant. 'Yes, Ethel, I nearly died a few years ago. There's nothing to fear. In fact it's beautiful. Just go into the light'.

Ethel squeezed Jenny's hand once more. 'I know dear, I know. I'm not afraid. I can see the light'.

Jenny remembered the brightest light she had ever experienced – a light that exuded unconditional love and acceptance. She knew Ethel could sense it too. Soon she would experience that same blissful place that she had once visited. Jenny felt a brief moment of yearning for that other-dimensional paradise'.

Ethel closed her eyes once more, mouthing incoherent words to invisible entities only she could see. Gradually, her movements slowed. Her breathing became shallow and Jenny knew the time had come. Soothingly, she held the old lady's hand, whispering reassuring words as she slipped into unconsciousness.

Soon Ethel was barely alive. Each intermittent breath rasped and gurgled as fluid pooled in her lungs. Her thin fingers fell limply away from Jenny's hand. Then she lay perfectly still, her final breath had been scarcely perceptible.

She had made her transition into death.

'Goodbye, Ethel. Be at peace', Jenny whispered, knowing that Ethel would be able to see her as she floated up from her body and into the tunnel that would transport her into another dimension of the universe. She was glad Ethel had been greeted by people she loved. Jenny knew she'd been ready and willing for death.

Jenny respectfully waited a few moments before she stood at the old lady's bedside. She glanced around the room at her photographs, the recorded memories of a lifetime now abandoned. Of one thing she was certain; that Ethel would see and feel the events of her life once more in a completely different way as she was welcomed into the blissful light. She vaguely remembered her own life review, although much of it had become hazy and she struggled to recall the details. Quietly, Jenny covered the old lady's lifeless face with a sheet and left the room, glad she'd been able to ease the suffering and loneliness of the last hours of her life.

'She's gone', Jenny said to the sister in charge of the shift. 'She was very peaceful at the end'.

'Thank you, Jenny. It was so good of you to stay with her. I'm sure she appreciated it. We'll lay her out in a while and call the funeral directors'. Sister Walters said with a grateful smile.

'OK – I'd better get home and relieve Katie's babysitter. Mike's not home for a few hours yet'. Jenny felt a touch of guilt at leaving her seven year old daughter with the babysitter again but she also felt a responsibility to her work. Ethel hadn't chosen to die on the day Mike was on call. Jenny often felt this awkward conflict. If she was at home, she felt she should be at work, nursing patients that needed her, yet if she was at work, she felt she should be at home with her daughter. It was a constant wrench on her conscience. Of course, Mike's job as acting consultant surgeon had to take priority. It was the main reason why Jenny had stayed with the nursing agency. At least she could fit in her shifts around everyone else and it mostly worked out well. Soon,

Katie would be back in school after the summer holidays and things would run a little more smoothly. She knew she had to make the most of the time that Katie was at home. She would plan something fun for them to do together.

'See you soon', sister said.

Jenny washed her hands and went into the changing room to get out of her nurses' scrubs and back into her jeans and t-shirt. It had been a sad but strangely rewarding day but now she was looking forward to getting home to her family. Jenny grabbed her bag, said a few goodbye's to some of the patients and nurses as she left the hospice and got into her car for the thirty minute drive home.

She'd sold her clapped out old Audi and replaced it with a stylish Citroen DS3 with a purple coloured trim. She needed a reliable car when Katie had been born, although the dogs hadn't wasted any time ruining the back seats. It hadn't seemed to matter to her. Jenny was becoming less concerned with material things as time went on. She'd noticed it in the months after her near death experience but over the past seven years, she could care less about fashion and all the latest gadgets and material things – things she'd loved and coveted in her youth. They were fairly comfortable financially and neither she nor Mike yearned for a more luxurious lifestyle. They were content in their modest seaside cottage where they'd created a home together.

Mike was very different from Bob, her ex, in that respect. Her life had turned out well. She now had a wonderful husband and an adorable little girl that they both loved to distraction. Bob was now firmly in the past – at least as far as she was concerned. Bob seemed to have a different view of things and worryingly had been calling her regularly during the past few months. He'd made it obvious he still cared about her. Yet Jenny felt completely detached from him. She was re-married now and it was too late for them – their time was over. He should have taken better care of their relationship when he'd had the chance. There was no way she'd give up her life with Mike and their daughter to resume what had been a conflicted and abusive relationship at times. She had tried her best but it was over and she wanted him to move on and let her live her life. She would have to be firmer with him, she vowed.

Jenny pulled onto the coast road that led to the village. She loved the familiar drive and opened her window to appreciate the freshness of the sea air. She drew in a deep breath and felt utter gratitude for her life. What seemed like a few short years ago she had almost died. Jenny had glimpsed the survival of consciousness after death and had desperately wanted to stay in the incredible love and acceptance she'd experienced in that other-worldly dimension – she'd even had moments when she wished she could return, just like she'd experienced that morning as Ethel passed had away. But mostly, she was glad she'd been persuaded that it was not her time to die and that she should go back into her body. As distressing as it had been at the time to return to the excruciating pain of her physical existence, she knew she was meant to live out this lifetime.

Somehow, she knew there were important events to come that would explain so much. Answers to burning questions that still hung in her mind...

Jenny drove along the coast, the open sea to her right. Gentle waves were rolling onto the sandy shore and the afternoon sun was low in the sky. She still marvelled at the fact that she lived in such an idyllic setting – her former life in London now felt like another lifetime.

Jenny reached her cottage and parked the Citroen outside. She could see Katie playing with the dogs in their new extension, which overlooked the sea. Life couldn't get much better, she thought. As well as a wonderful husband and a beautiful and talented daughter, she had a rewarding career. She let herself into the cottage and little Katie ran toward her, arms wide open for a hug with her mother. Treacle, Mike's black Labrador, was following close behind. Jenny threw her coat and bag onto a chair and embraced her daughter as she fell into her arms. She kissed her cheek and pulled her closer. 'My gorgeous girl, how are you today?'

'Great Mum – we made ice cream and I painted some pictures for you'. Katie said excitedly.

Treacle bounded up to Jenny, almost bowling her over in his eagerness to greet her. 'Hello, Treacle, you daft thing', Jenny said, playfully patting the dog. He panted a greeting, revelling in the attention before leaping off to fetch his ball.

Barney, Jenny's Doberman, struggled to get down from his place on the sofa. His old arthritic joints were obviously painful at times but he was determined to greet her as he always had. He limped over to Jenny and she hugged him too, his coat as soft and shiny as ever. Jenny and Katie stroked him together as Katie animatedly told her mother about her day.

Honey, Mike's golden Labrador, stayed in her basket in the kitchen. She was heavily pregnant and had spent most of her time lately just resting and sleeping. She lifted her head and wagged her tail to acknowledge Jenny's return home, then grunted and returned to her snooze.

Laura, Katie's babysitter, appeared in the kitchen doorway. 'Hello Jenny, how did it go at the hospice today?' Laura was a delightful woman in her early thirties. She was always happy to go over and above the call of duty with anything that was required of her.

Jenny valued her highly. With Mike working long hours building his surgical career, she needed someone reliable to support with childcare if she was to continue with her nursing work. 'Hello Laura,' she said, 'Ethel is finally at rest and I was glad I was there for her. Thanks for helping out again at short notice. How was your day? Sounds like you had fun.'

'Yes it was lovely. We took Treacle and Barney to the beach and made ice cream and then Katie painted some pictures for you, didn't you Katie?' Laura smiled at the little girl.

Katie nodded in reply, her face beaming with joy as she went off to find her pictures.

'Any more shifts coming up?' Laura asked.

'Thankfully I have a day off tomorrow but I still have those shifts on the surgical ward and theatre coming up the rest of the week – the rota is on the calendar. Actually, it will be lovely to work with Mike for a change – we seem to be like ships that pass in the night lately.' Jenny rolled her eyes. It was a rare thing to have a family day all together so that they could make the most of Katie's school holidays.

'I know what you mean,' Laura said. 'If you need me, you know where I am but I will be here the day after tomorrow as planned. I was thinking of taking Katie to the zoo.'

'She'll love that,' Jenny said, a tinge of guilt that she couldn't take her daughter to the zoo herself.

'OK, I'll get off now. Have a nice day off tomorrow!' Laura collected her things and said goodbye to Katie who was searching through her paintings in the conservatory, Treacle and Barney were lying on the oak flooring close by.

Jenny wandered out to the kitchen to make a well-earned mug of coffee. She stopped to stroke Honey's head. The pups would be born soon, she thought. She took her coffee into the conservatory – the new extension that they used mostly as a family sitting room. One wall was entirely glass and boasted glorious sea views from the cliff top. Jenny marvelled at the dynamic landscape of the coast. It was ever-changing depending on the weather and the state of the tide. Even in the depths of winter, she loved to sit and watch the sea, spotting seabirds through her binoculars. She'd even seen dolphins on a few occasions and grey seals sometimes visited the area, especially along the more rugged coastline to the east. Jenny sank into the white cotton covered sofa, the full panoramic view in front of her. Barney and Treacle settled at her feet. The tide was part way up the beach and a flight of cormorants flew past the cliff edge. Jenny could hear the gulls screeching in the distance. It was good to be home…

Katie had found her painting and sat next to Jenny to show off her artwork. 'This is excellent Katie', Jenny said as she admired the child's painting of a house. Katie was just seven years old but her artwork was remarkably mature for her age. Jenny knew she'd make a talented artist.

'It's your house, Mum. You know the one you lived in before I was born'. Katie smiled at her mother.

Jenny looked at the picture. It was a large double-fronted detached house with a bushy tree to the right and a blue front door. It didn't look like any house she'd ever lived in. 'Actually, Katie, I lived in a flat in London before you were born. Are you thinking of someone else – Dad's house perhaps?' Jenny put her arm around Katie as she snuggled up to her.

'No Mum, it's *your* old house. It's only in the next village – don't you remember it? You didn't like it there'. Katie was adamant.

Jenny looked again at the details of the painting, trying to find something familiar. There was what looked like a low stone wall along the front of the house with a central gate. The house itself was white – possibly rendered – with the typical symmetrical Georgian styling of the windows on either side of a central porch. On the right of the pitched slate roof was a distinctive attic window with a face pencilled in behind. Jenny didn't recognise the house at all. 'No sorry, Katie, I don't recognise it. Could it be one of your friends from school that live there?'

'No Mum, I *told* you it's *your* house. Look there you are in the window'. Katie pointed to the sad-looking face behind the attic window.

Jenny was puzzled. Katie must be getting mixed up with something she'd seen in a book or on television. There was no way she'd have lived in a detached house as opulent-looking as this. It was nothing like any house she'd lived in as a child either. Her parents had always lived in a three story Victorian terraced property in Bath – it had been left to them by her maternal grandmother. And anyway, how would Katie possibly know about a home Jenny had lived in before she was even born? Jenny had never been back to London since she'd left nearly a decade ago and she knew Katie hadn't been there. It was just a child's fertile imagination...

Katie seemed exasperated that Jenny couldn't remember the house. 'Mum – it *was* your house before I was born. Not this time – last time'.

'What do you mean, last time? You were only born once!' Jenny was amused at Katie's make believe story.

'No it was when I was born *before*!' Katie emphasised her point.

'You're being silly now', Jenny said, sure that Katie's imagination was working overtime.

Katie grabbed the painting and stomped off to her bedroom muttering under her breath.

Jenny sighed and sipped her coffee. She was too tired to think about it or go after Katie. Her day at the hospice had been long and tiring. She just needed some peace to take in the view and recharge her batteries. Mike would be home soon and she would have to prepare dinner for them all and get Katie ready for bed. She felt a pang of guilt at not listening to Katie. She'd been at work all day and her daughter had missed her mother's company but at this moment, she just needed ten minutes to herself. Sometimes the demands of working full time and being a mother and a wife were exhausting. She loved her family more than anything in the world but her needs seemed to be constantly at the bottom of a long list of priorities.

Just let me have ten minutes, she thought as she sipped her coffee...

Thirty minutes later, Jenny wearily dragged herself up from the sofa and headed into the kitchen to start preparing their evening meal. She called to Katie from the bottom of the stairs. 'Katie, are you alright? Come and talk to me while I get dinner ready'. She waited a few moments for a reply.

Jenny heard a thump and Katie running across her bedroom floor. She was cheeringly calling back to her. 'OK, Mum, I'm coming'.

She made her way down the steep stairs of the cottage and joined Jenny in the kitchen. Without the need for words, mother and daughter exchanged a look that said all was forgiven. Jenny smoothed her daughter's silky blonde hair and smiled. It was just normal family life.

Jenny cooked and Katie helped lay the table with knives and forks and spoons for the ice cream desert she'd made with Laura earlier. They chatted about the antics of the dogs and excitedly anticipated the arrival of Honey's puppies that were due any day. They had decided as a family that Honey could have puppies and that *maybe* they could keep one. There had been no promises, but Jenny knew it would be practically impossible for her to resist and that Katie would be bitterly disappointed if she couldn't keep at least one. They'd been making a never-ending list of names for the pups.

Barney limped into the kitchen to see what the excitement was about; arthritis making his legs stiff and painful. He was looking quite old these days, Jenny thought. He was nearly nine after all. She wasn't sure how he'd take to a litter of boisterous pups but he was a good natured dog and she would make sure he had his own space to get some peace and quiet in his old age. Perhaps the pups would keep him young, she thought. She loved the Doberman as much as ever – they had been through a lot together over the years. Katie loved him too. She had grown up with Barney around and she was turning into a devoted animal lover like her parents.

Just as the meal was ready, Mike appeared in the hallway and Katie and Treacle rushed out to greet him. The usual excited hugs and kisses ensued but when the fuss died down and Jenny had her turn, she could see he looked tired and drawn.

Mike hugged her tightly as if he'd never let go.

'Are you OK, Mike?' Jenny asked, sensing something wasn't right.

'I'll tell you when Katie's in bed', he said, finally releasing her.

Throughout the meal, Jenny watched her husband. She was concerned but recognised that it was something he didn't want to discuss in front of Katie. He was trying to be upbeat and chatty with his daughter but Jenny sensed a deep sadness underlying his demeanour. Since her near death experience, her intuition had become considerably heightened and she readily picked up on the feelings of others; especially those closest to her.

'Yum, yum, gorgeous ice cream, Katie', Mike said, licking the bowl exaggeratedly after it was all gone. 'You'll have to make some more'.

Katie laughed at her father's comedy antics. 'Yes and we'll have chocolate next time', she said, giggling.

Finally, Jenny felt Mike was ready to talk over what was troubling him and she got Katie to bed. 'Come on munchkin, let have a quick story and get you to bed. We'll do something nice together tomorrow'.

Katie reached up, kissed her father goodnight and happily went up to her bedroom with Jenny. She picked a short story from her book of fairy tales and Jenny sat on the bed and read it to her. Before she reached the end, Katie had fallen asleep. Jenny tucked her in, tenderly kissed her forehead and turned off the light, leaving the curtains open a crack to allow a slither of moonlight into the room. She closed the door and went down to find Mike clearing the dinner table and loading the dishwasher.

'She's asleep', Jenny said, 'she's had a busy day with Laura'.

Mike turned to face Jenny, his green eyes welling up with tears.

She moved toward him. 'What is it? What's happened?'

'I called in to see Dad on the way home. He told me he's got cancer'. Mike looked ashen, obviously shocked at the news. Jenny knew how much he loved and admired his father. He would be devastated.

'Oh my God', Jenny said, searching his face for more information.

'It's in his liver and it's inoperable – the tumour is way too big'. Mike was shaking his head, barely able to believe the news.

Jenny was stunned. How could this be – this gentle, intelligent man who been such a wonderful father to Mike, the perfect father-in-law to her and a much loved grandfather to Katie.

'Can't he have chemo to reduce the tumour?' Jenny felt desperate to find a solution.

'He said he's had several rounds of Avastin, Oxaliplatin and fluorouracil. It's the strongest cocktail of chemo they have'. Mike said.

'Ah yes the affectionately known FU2. Surely that will kill the cancer?' Jenny asked.

'Apparently it's not working. The tumour hasn't shrunk at all and he's had enough of the side-effects. He's been fine on chemo weekends because of the steroids and all the other medications to counter side effects like nausea. But it's after the treatment he's really suffering. He been having severe flu-like symptoms and his throat is really painful. He says it's like being scratched with razor blades. But I think it's the fatigue that's doing it – it's just too much for him'. Mike said. 'He's stopped the treatment'.

'How long has he known about this?' Jenny asked. 'He seemed fine the other week when I saw him'.

'He had a diagnosis about four months ago', Mike said. 'He said he didn't want to distract me from my career while I'm acting as consultant. I wish he'd told me, Jenny. He's more important to me that my bloody career. And you know Mum, she just goes along with anything he says – she was sworn to secrecy'.

Jenny nodded. Martha was a loyal wife. 'She must be distraught', Jenny said.

'I think she is underneath but you know what she's like – good at putting on a façade of being able to cope. The pair of them just seem to be accepting it. I'm not sure that I can be so philosophical though'. Mike shook his head, obviously finding it hard to take in the news.

Jenny was shattered. It was unthinkable that her wonderful father-in-law was going to die.

It was way too soon to lose him…

'Jenny, he's got six months if he's lucky'. A single tear bulged onto Mike's cheek.

They both fell into to one another's arms and sobbed…

Chapter three: revelations

Reverend Wheelan opened the morning mail. He knew one letter was from the Synod because of its distinctive envelope. He'd been half expecting it and sure enough, the letter informed him that his chapel had been singled out for closure. He was now semi-retired as a chapel minister and the congregation was too small to be worth keeping it open – they would have to go elsewhere in the circuit. Costly repairs were needed and it was to be sold off at auction. Wheelan had a matter of months' notice to quit and move out.

'Fucking marvellous' – after all the years of service he'd put in. Wheelan felt he'd been well and truly snubbed by the church authorities. But he'd seen it coming for a long time and already had a plan in place. He had decided to buy the chapel and the manse himself. It had been his home for most of his adult life and besides, he had far too many secrets attached to this place. Where would he go anyway? He liked the area and where else would he get to live right on the beach in a deserted beauty spot like this?

It was an easy decision.

He would use the stash of money he'd made from his drug dealing and buy both properties outright. It would completely wipe him out financially but he had a small pension to live on and he'd own his home. Buying the chapel as well – even if it lay empty and crumbling would prevent anyone developing it. He couldn't face having neighbours of any description after all the years he'd enjoyed his solitude there. If anyone asked where he'd gotten the money, he could say he'd won it on the horses or inherited it – it didn't really matter – he was well used to lying to cover his tracks. He was looking forward to having security in his retirement. He even planned to 'retire' from dealing drugs. His customers had dwindled as they craved more fashionable designer drugs offered by anonymous black market sellers online. Wheelan found it hard to keep up. It had really been Morgan's business, after all. He had only ever dabbled on the side. He seemed to be left with were the opportunistic pilferers who thought they could get their hands on his merchandise for free. Only one way to deal with them, he thought wryly…

Wheelan decided he could no longer face the low-life villains he had to do business with, especially after yesterday's episode. He didn't relish the thought of having to kill again. Much as it gave him immense pleasure to take the life of that thieving yob, he wasn't planning to take up killing as a new career.

Yes, he would buy both properties. It would take just a few phone calls and the deed would be done. Wheelan set to work to finalise the arrangements that would see him owning the chapel and the manse complete with the modest amount of land that included the graveyard. His secrets would be safe.

Wheelan made the necessary arrangements to transfer ownership of the properties to him and by lunchtime, Mary had appeared at the door. He wasn't sure if she was going to come back after their little spat the day before but she turned up as usual to tidy up and cook his lunch. Some days she'd arrive at midday and be gone a few hours later; some days she'd arrive during the late afternoon to cook dinner and some days she'd leave him to his own devices. They had a workable arrangement and Wheelan usually knew exactly when to expect her. She was reliable if nothing else.

'Hello Reverend', Mary said brusquely as she walked through the front door. This new formality told Wheelan she was annoyed with him.

Hello Mary – are you OK?' Wheelan offered.

'Oh yes – I'm just fine.' She said. But there was a tone about her voice that betrayed a superior attitude. It was as if she felt she had the upper hand with him.

Wheelan knew that tone and it meant trouble. Mary would brood about things for a long time before it finally spilled out and he would usually have to suffer the consequences in the meantime. He chose to ignore it.

Wheelan reached for an envelope in the dresser in the hall and handed it to her. 'Here's your pay, Mary. I forgot to give it to you yesterday'. He thought that might soften her up.

Mary said a curt 'thank you' as she took it from him and tucked it into her handbag. She pushed past him in the hall and began to tidy up the dishes in the kitchen. 'Sandwiches for lunch.' She said flatly.

Wheelan knew she was irritated with him. She usually cooked for him but today it was obviously too much trouble for her. 'That's fine Mary, thanks'. He tried not to make things worse by being contrary and he was at least man enough to take his punishment from her.

Wheelan hesitated to follow her into the kitchen. He wanted to make peace with her but at the same time avoid any further confrontation – or worse give her any reason to think he'd changed his mind about the status of their relationship, or rather lack of it. He decided to stay out of her way and went into the siting room at the front of the manse. The sound of his father's antique clock ticked soothingly and he strode over to the window to gaze at his much-loved view of the sea.

On the beach he saw a young girl with her dog. It was Kate Halliday from Seagull Cottage and that wretched

Doberman of theirs. He must be ancient by now, Wheelan thought. He absently rubbed his leg where the dog had bitten him in the cave years before. The damned scar still ached now and again and he cursed the dog under his breath. He hoped they wouldn't call in today – he really wasn't in the mood for that.

'OK, come and get it!' Mary called from the kitchen. She liked him to eat at the table. She said he was a messy eater.

'Coming', Wheelan dutifully shouted back as he turned to make his way into the kitchen. He generally complied with her wishes for a quiet life when she was there but ate wherever he liked when she wasn't.

Wheelan sat at his usual seat at the kitchen table and Mary plonked a plate of sandwiches down in front of him and poured him a steaming mug of tea. He felt like a naughty schoolboy. He looked up at her to thank her. Her face was stern and set into a dour grimace. She definitely had on one of her holier-than-thou attitudes. He was in trouble. Wheelan quietly ate his sandwiches, following her around the room with his eyes as she busied herself with a mop and bucket.

Wheelan suddenly recoiled as he tasted the filling of his sandwich. He couldn't tell what the hell it was but it tasted bitter. She was watching him, so he just swallowed, not wanting to irritate her further. He knew it was ridiculous, but Mary had a way of guilting him into conforming to her demands. One look from her was enough. It reminded him of the way his mother had disciplined him when he was young and weirdly, he found it comforting.

The sandwiches tasted disgusting. Was Mary getting some sort of childish revenge by making him eat something revolting? Was she waiting for him to say something? He wasn't going to. He finished the lot and sat quietly sipping his tea.

He was about to start a conversation to cover up the tense atmosphere between them when the doorbell rang. Mary put down her mop and went to answer it.

'Hello Katie!' Wheelan heard Mary greet the little girl.

Shit, he thought, he'd have to put up with this as well now. He hated Kate's visits but as a chapel minister he felt obliged to be pleasant – it was an act he'd perfected over the years. Why she felt the need to visit him all the time, he couldn't fathom but at least Mary was here to make conversation with her and he could take a back seat. With any luck it would smooth things over between them as well. Mary had taken to the girl – she said she reminded her of 'their Kate'. He wasn't so sure.

He took a deep breath in readiness – there was no escape...

Katie came into the kitchen with the Doberman at her side. His head reached up to her waist and he was very protective of her, always staying close. Mary followed behind, fussing over them like a mother hen. Wheelan forced a smile and greeted the little girl as Mary offered her a seat at the kitchen table opposite him. He looked down at the dog and the Doberman glowered back, his lip quivering as if he was about to snarl. Wheelan narrowed his eyes at him, daring him to make a move. The dog got the message and backed down. He lay on the kitchen floor next to Katie. They went through this tired routine every time...

Mary poured Kate a drink of lemonade and fished out a couple of biscuits from the tin. They chatted about school and the dogs. Katie was animated as she told them that Honey was expecting puppies any day and soon the atmosphere lifted. Wheelan reluctantly chipped in with his own pleasantries when he was prompted to by Mary. He couldn't help wondering why this kid kept coming to visit. Was she spying on him? Did her mother send her to see what he was up to? Perhaps Jenny's memory was coming back and she remembered the incident in the cave. But that was years ago before she cracked her head and nearly died. Would she remember that? He didn't know but it bothered him sometimes. He guessed it was lucky really that the stupid mutt *had* bitten him or things could have been much worse...

'Well, it was lovely to see you Katie, and you Barney', Mary was saying as the girl finally stood to leave. Wheelan's mind had gone off into a daydream but quickly jumped back to attention.

The Doberman struggled to get up from the floor, his claws slipping on the tiles. Yes, the damned flea-bag was looking old these days, Wheelan mused. I bet he wouldn't attack me so ferociously now. Barney still managed to growl at Wheelan. He knew the dog hadn't forgotten...

Soon Katie and Barney were gone and Mary came back to resume her mopping, a smile on her face at last. Wheelan was relieved. Perhaps now things could go back to normal. Wheelan stood up to return to his armchair in the living room. He was halfway through a good book he wanted to finish.

Just as he settled himself down to read, he felt a sharp pain in his stomach. For a few moments, he was doubled up in agony but it did slowly subside. Those bloody sandwiches, Wheelan thought, what the fuck did she put in them? He thought better than to ask her. Maybe it wasn't just childish revenge – perhaps she was trying to poison him, he thought sarcastically. He'd have to make it up to her or there'd be more of the same to come. He knew Mary could string out a grievance for days.

He got back to his book and could hear Mary clattering in the kitchen as she prepared his dinner for later. He hoped she'd gotten over any feelings of revenge she'd had or he'd be making his own meals.

An hour later, Mary popped her head around the door of the sitting room. 'I'm off now – it's pasta for your dinner – you just have to heat it up in the microwave'. Her tone was business-like as she reverted to being 'just a housekeeper'. It was an act she put on to let him know she was upset with him. Still, it was better than the silent treatment or the over-familiarity of late, he thought.

'OK, thank you Mary', Wheelan said, donning his best clergyman's smile in a pathetic attempt to win her over.

Mary looked at him as if to say, 'yes you can smile but I've got the measure of you and you'd better watch your step'. With that, she was gone.

Wheelan watched her drive away and sighed. He was getting too old for all this. He felt like he was treading on eggshells and having to please everyone all the time – even in his own home. He'd felt that way for most of his life. That's why he'd gotten himself into so much trouble; especially with Morgan's blackmail all over the years. His act as a caring minister had been exhausting at times and he was glad the chapel was closing. Perhaps now he could enjoy his retirement in peace.

Wheelan saw Mary's car disappear up the slipway to the main road and he couldn't resist a look at the dinner she'd left for him. He hauled himself out of the armchair and went out to the kitchen counter. He lifted the lid off the casserole dish and recoiled at the pungent smell. He loved pasta and had it often but this was repulsive. What the hell was she up to, he thought. This was taking things a bit too far. For God's sake, couldn't she accept that he didn't want her fawning over him like a love-sick teenager. Was there any need to treat him like this? Wheelan scraped the foul-smelling food into the pedal bin at the side of the sink. There was no way he'd be eating that.

Maybe she *was* poisoning him…

The thought stuck in Wheelan's mind and he couldn't help himself thinking the worst. He powered up his laptop and began searching for information about poisoning on the Internet. There were some horrendous cases of fatal poisoning and intriguingly gruesome stories about Russian spies being killed with exotic sounding chemicals but his attention fixed onto a website that described Munchhausen's syndrome, a condition where people fake illness in order to get sympathy and attention. He was most interested in Munchhausen's by Proxy – where people make others ill in order to gain sympathy for themselves or to cause someone to become dependent on them. It was most prevalent in mothers who cause symptoms in their children but it had been known in adults too. Poisoning was one of the commonest methods.

Wheelan was aghast. The description fitted Mary and her behaviour perfectly. She could be making him ill so that he would become dependent on her and she would have her wish – that they would be together as a couple. She knew he hated consulting the doctor. She must be feeling confident she'd get away with it, he thought.

Then he looked up the symptoms of poisoning. It couldn't be strychnine. It acted too rapidly and he certainly wasn't convulsing, having seizures or asphyxiating as the website described. He read with horror as it described how the victim, after ingesting strychnine, would jack-knife dramatically back and forth followed by furious and savage convulsions. He anxiously felt his pulse. Surely it couldn't be strychnine, he thought.

But the description he read next hit him like a bolt out of the blue.

Arsenic!

He was feeling nauseous, had stomach pain, a dry mouth and had been vomiting. That's it. Mary was poisoning him with arsenic. It was also relatively easy to get hold of. He read on to discover how the victim of arsenic poisoning would finally haemorrhage from the intestine, the loss of fluids resulting in vascular collapse, dizziness, convulsions, coma and death.

Wheelan's blood ran cold.

That's it! She was poisoning him slowly with arsenic to make him dependent on her. It explained his worsening symptoms over the past few months and of course – the way he'd vomited after the cake she'd made the evening before. There had been that nasty metallic taste. It must have been arsenic poisoning. That must have been why she didn't offer Kate a slice of cake as she normally would. It was poisoned...

He froze with horror.

There was no way he was ever eating anything she prepared for him again.

He reached for the whiskey. He had to think.

He poured himself a very large single malt and sat staring out of the window, his mind awash with terrifying images of his demise. It was mid-afternoon and the tide was almost full out. The beach was deserted. What the hell should he do? Should he confront Mary and ask her outright if she was poisoning him? That would obviously provoke an argument. He needed to know the truth and she wasn't going to admit she was deliberately poisoning him. He had to concoct a plan to catch her out. Then he could confront her when he had all the evidence.

He took a large swig of his drink. A burning pain shot down his oesophagus and he winced in agony. A couple more of these and he wouldn't notice the pain. Wheelan knew full well the alcohol wasn't helping but he couldn't quit the habit of a lifetime. Not now. It had always dulled the monotonous reality of his life, but now he needed it to steady his nerves.

Wheelan sat in his armchair where he desperately tried to think of a plan to get Mary to admit she'd been feeding him arsenic. What could he do? He could have his food tested – he was sure there were laboratories somewhere where he could get that done. That would be his evidence. He could go to his doctor and get some tests done. He could go to the police. No – not the police. He had too much to hide. There had to be something he could do to catch her out without going through any of that. It would take too long.

Wheelan scanned the Internet and swigged his whisky for the next two hours. His mind was racing. He was convinced Mary was out to poison him, make him an invalid, so she could keep him a prisoner in his own home. He had to stop her…

'Fuck it', he said finally.

Wheelan stood, wobbling as he tried to balance. He'd drunk far too much but was determined to take action. He'd put up with enough from Mary and he was going to man up and put a stop to it once and for all. This was the last straw.

Wheelan staggered out to the hall, grabbing a jacket from the coat stand as he went. He fumbled, but failing to get his arm into the sleeve, he abandoned the jacket, dropping it in a heap on the floor.

His head was swimming and it wasn't just the alcohol.

He grabbed his keys and made for the front door. A blast of cool air greeted him as he stepped outside and slammed the door behind him.

Almost tripping over his own feet, he walked over to the Landy – a newer model of his favourite old car. Scrabbling for the right key, he got in and started the engine, revving fiendishly as he tried repeatedly to engage the gearstick.

He was drunk – he was aware of that – but he had to put a stop to Mary's activities. He was convinced she was making him ill and he had to confront her.

His confidence buoyed by alcohol, he drove off, gravel flying in all directions as he sped down the driveway toward the slipway. He turned to climb the slope and pushed the accelerator hard to the floor as he reached the steepest part of the hill. His vision was blurred and he shook his head in a futile effort to focus on the road ahead.

He turned right at the main road, almost scraping a lamppost as he went. He mounted the kerb briefly as he straightened out and drove furiously toward the next village a few miles along the coast. His driving was erratic but miraculously, he managed to make headway toward Mary's cottage.

Wheelan was relying on his knowledge of the road more than on what he could see through the windscreen. Everything was blurred into double vision. The Landy swerved from one side of the road to the other as he sped toward his destination.

He vaguely noticed another car as it veered into the hedge to avoid him, the driver blasting the car's horn angrily at him, but he carried on, determined to confront Mary.

Incredibly, he made it, pulling up outside the small stone cottage on the outskirts of the village. He parked the Landy awkwardly on the grass verge and almost fell out of the car as he headed for Mary's front door.

He banged loudly on the door and within seconds, it opened. Mary stood there startled, her eyes wide with astonishment.

'Lucas – are you alright?' she said. She grabbed him by the shoulders as he almost stumbled over the doorstep. 'You'd better come in'. She said, guiding him into the sitting room. As he lurched forward into her, she pushed him onto the sofa. He could barely stand and reeked of whiskey.

Mary loomed over him as he rubbed his temples, trying to focus and shake off the effects of the alcohol.

'I think you need some strong coffee. You've obviously been hitting the bottle again. Shame on you.' Mary sounded like a school teacher, scolding a naughty boy. She turned to go and make the coffee.

'No wait', Wheelan said, grabbing her wrist. He looked up, her face a picture of disgust. 'I know what you're trying to do – you're trying to poison me'. Wheelan was slurring his words badly.

'What on earth are you on about Lucas?' Mary asked, completely stunned at his accusation.

'You're poisoning me with arsenic so I'll need you'. Wheelan stared at Mary, trying hard to focus as he waited for a reaction.

'You're talking utter rubbish. You're drunk.' Mary tried to pull her arm away.

'No I'm right', Wheelan said, clasping her arm more tightly, 'it's called munchers or something – I researched it on the Internet. You're putting arsenic in my food'.

'Don't be so ridiculous', Mary said, firmly pulling her arm away from him. 'I'm going to make you some strong coffee and you can jolly well sober up'. With that she was gone.

Wheelan slumped back into the sofa, his head spinning.

Within seconds, he'd fallen asleep.

+++

Three hours later, Wheelan woke up on Mary's sofa. She'd covered him with one of her hand-knitted woollen blankets and was sitting in her armchair watching a sloppy romance on television. She looked calm, Wheelan thought as he gradually recalled what had happened.

Shit, he thought, why had he been so stupid? The bloody whiskey again... Why did he never learn his lesson?

Wheelan tried to waken fully. His head hurt, his mouth was dry and he felt sick again. He rubbed his eyes, the rough skin of his hands like sandpaper on his eyelids.

Mary turned her head to face him. 'Ah, you're back with us then? I hope you've sobered up'.

Wheelan nodded lamely.

'There's a drink on the table next to you'. Mary said bluntly as she turned her attention back to the film.

Wheelan hesitated. Should he drink something Mary had prepared? He glanced across. It was a glass of water. His throat was dry and he felt like hell, so he reached for it, sniffed it and tasted a small drop. It did taste like water. He desperately needed a drink, so he chanced it and took a mouthful.

He sat up and pushed the blanket off, 'Mary...' he started to explain why he'd driven over to her house the worse for drink but she cut him off.

'Lucas', she said, turning fully in her chair to face him, 'I'm certainly not poisoning you, though God knows I've wanted to sometimes. You *can* be a cantankerous old bugger.' Mary hesitated to say more.

'Well it just seemed to fit what's been happening...' Wheelan said, suddenly feeling foolish. Had he jumped the gun? Probably. That would be typical of him, he thought.

'What do you mean?' Mary asked.

Wheelan swallowed another mouthful of water before he went on. 'I've been feeling quite ill lately and you've been getting all mawkish on me. I was as sick as a dog after that cake and – well, I don't know, it just seemed obvious to me earlier on'. Wheelan saw no reaction from Mary. She just observed him steadily, her eyes darkening, becoming more serious.

Wheelan was confused – he had to know the truth. 'Tell me honestly, Mary. Have you been putting something in my food?'

Mary leaned toward him, her face morphing into the expression he'd seen that morning as she left. It was that holier-than-thou face he'd seen so many times before. 'I don't need to poison you Lucas – I have something far more interesting that will keep *you* under control'. She paused, her eyes steadily watching his reaction.

Wheelan frowned. 'What do you mean?'

'I know all about your evil drug dealing. It's been going on for years'.

Wheelan felt a shot of adrenaline flash through his veins. Good God – he hadn't expected that.

'And don't blame Terry Morgan – he's been dead for nearly nine years now and you're still up to no good. I've known all along what you were up to. I've got enough evidence on you to have you put away for life'. Mary sat back triumphantly, her expression telling him she meant it.

Wheelan was stunned. How the bloody hell could she have known? Had she been snooping? Had she found something to incriminate him? She'd never indicated she knew anything before now.

'Like I said, Lucas, I know you far better than you think'. Mary smirked as she turned her attention nonchalantly back to the television.

She obviously thinks she's got the upper hand, Wheelan thought. But how does she know? What does she intend to do now? Wheelan's heart sank. He thought he was free from Morgan's blackmail now he was dead but this was too much. He'd seen Mary practically every day for all these years yet he had no inkling about what she knew. She was as deceptive as he was, he thought.
'How did you find out?' Wheelan asked, knowing it was useless to try to deny it.

Mary was silent for a few moments before answering, almost reluctant to give away her secret. 'Terry and I had an arrangement'.

'What arrangement? What are you talking about? Wheelan could barely believe what had just transpired.

Then Mary's gaze was steadily watching him once again. 'He wanted me to keep an eye on you and he paid me very well for my services'.

Dear God. All this time and Mary had been in on Morgan's blackmail. He'd had no inkling whatsoever. He was beginning to think that Mary was a bigger hypocrite and a far better liar than he was to have kept the secret all this time.

'So what exactly do you know?' Wheelan asked.

'Everything, my dear. Everything'. Mary smirked again. This time she looked directly at him.

Wheelan was stunned by this revelation. Mary and Morgan had been in cahoots and he was the victim of their conspiracy to keep him under control. How the hell hadn't he realised before now?

He could see why Mary was so confident. She was using her knowledge to persuade him – force him – to get closer. What the hell did she see in him? She must love the feeling of power she had over him. That must be it. Maybe she wasn't poisoning him but what she knew gave her that air of superiority she showed whenever there was friction between them. He'd been a total mug all this time.

Wheelan suddenly felt the need to escape. He wanted the sanctuary of his home and solitude to think. He was confused and shocked. He needed space to plan his next move.

'I have to go', he said, pushing himself forward in his seat.

'OK – drive carefully'. Mary said as she put her chubby hand on his knee, giving it an affectionate rub. 'I'll see you tomorrow as usual'. She smiled at him but it was a self-satisfied, sarcastic smile. She knew she was dominating the situation now.

Wheelan stood and brushed past her. He had to get out. His head was throbbing and his throat was raspingly dry. He wanted to get home and try to make sense of all that had happened.

Wheelan drove home in the dark, his mind numb. He had no idea what he would do next. But there was one thing nagging at him…

If she knew everything, did Mary also know about the murders he'd committed?

Chapter four: family

The morning sunlight diffused through the flimsy curtains as Jenny lay awake in bed; a heavy sadness filled her heart. The evening before had been an emotional one to say the least. Jenny knew that Mike was deeply shocked at the news of his father's terminal cancer and she too was having trouble believing it. John Halliday had been her rock while she'd been pregnant and he'd even delivered Katie – he was a kind man and she'd grown to love and admire him. He was a consultant obstetrician and a good one at that. It would be a tragic loss, not just for his family but for his patients too if he died so prematurely. And what about Martha, Mike's mother? Jenny knew she'd be utterly devastated to lose her husband after nearly fifty years of marriage, despite her outward pretence of coping. They'd always been a solid couple and Jenny knew they loved each other deeply.

She had to go and see them.

Jenny looked over at Mike. He was still sleeping next to her. Her heart went out to him. He had always been close to his father and was obviously distraught at the news. Was there really nothing that could be done? She knew Mike, as a surgeon, would do everything in his power to save his father if he could. Perhaps a second opinion was in order. Perhaps surgery could be an option after all. They could discuss it later. Mike also had a rare day off and although they'd planned a nice trip out with Katie, things were different now.

Jenny quietly got up and snuggled into her dressing gown. She'd make them both a cup of tea and see what Katie was up to. They were late getting up after the turmoil of the evening before and they'd had a restless night's sleep. She looked into Katie's room but she wasn't there. Downstairs, there was no sign of Barney but Honey was sleeping in her basket and Treacle was stretched out on the conservatory floor. Jenny found a note on the kitchen table.

'Dear Mum and Dad, Gone to the beach with Barney', it said succinctly in light blue crayon.

Jenny smiled. Her little daughter was growing up fast. She loved to be independent and she and Barney often went for walks on their own together. She'd had strict instructions to stick to the slipway to the beach and not venture onto the road, even though the traffic was sparse going through the village and that tucked-away part of the beach was generally quiet. Treacle was far too boisterous for her to handle by herself and Mike had forbidden her to take him. Barney, though, was gentle and quiet in his old age and the pair had an unbreakable bond of love and affection. Katie often sat in the kitchen alone with Barney and they would listen to her talking to the dog and telling him long stories – it was endearing.

Jenny made two mugs of strong tea and took them upstairs to bed, drawing the curtains back to reveal a spectacular open view of the coast. The tide was way down the beach and the sun was bright in a cloudless blue sky. Mike was waking up and rolled over to peer at Jenny, his hair dishevelled, eyes blinking against the light. He looked so vulnerable – not at all like the charismatic surgeon he was at work.

'Tea?' Jenny asked as she sat on the bed, handing him a mug.

'Great, thanks, love', Mike took it from her, his voice croaky from sleep.

'Katie's gone to the beach with Barney – she left a note'.

'That's nice', he said sipping his tea.

'How are you feeling this morning?' Jenny asked.

Mike sighed, 'I can still hardly believe it. Dad seems so strong and healthy – it doesn't seem possible that he's going to die so soon'.

'I know', Jenny said, 'he hasn't been ill – or at least he's not admitted to it. Do you think there's a chance he could be treated?'

'He said he'd looked at all the options. He's had a second opinion already and apparently there was nothing they could do. I'd like to have a chat with his oncologist though. I'd hate to see Dad giving up if there's the slightest chance'. Mike looked up at Jenny, his green eyes heavy with sadness but there was also a hint of hope.

'Shall we go and see them today? I'm sure Katie will be happy to do that instead of a day out. Laura's taking her to the zoo tomorrow anyway'. Jenny was keen to see John and Martha and make sure they were coping with the news. Her experience at the hospice might well be needed to care for her father-in-law when the time came and she wanted to do all she could to support them both.

'Yes, that's a good idea. I can't focus on anything else at the moment anyway. Should we tell Katie, do you think?' Mike sat up to finish his tea.

'Let's leave it for now. I think we'll handle it better once we've all got used to the idea. Let's see them today and make a judgement on it then'. Jenny was reluctant to give Katie the bad news that her beloved grandfather was going to die. She knew it was inevitable and that she'd need to spend time with him but today it all seemed too overwhelming.

'I think you're right, let's wait', Mike said. He reached for her hand. 'It'll be tough but we'll all get through it'.

Jenny smiled and took his hand. 'Yes we will'. She felt a surge of love for her husband. He'd been so kind and caring when she'd nearly died. He was a truly compassionate doctor and she knew he would be there for his father come what may.

They exchanged an affectionate kiss and Jenny went to shower and dress, leaving Mike to ponder his thoughts as he lingered in their cosy bed. She gazed at her reflection in the bathroom mirror, her hair tousled from sleep. She knew that death wasn't the end of her conscious existence and she felt that maybe it was the right time to tell Mike about her near death experience. If he realised that life continued after death, perhaps he'd be able to cope better with the loss of his father. Yet she was still reluctant to admit what had happened to her. Mike was sceptical and pragmatic and she wasn't sure he'd believe her or accept what she would tell him. Perhaps it wasn't the time to discuss death when there was still a glimmer of hope. Mike had only just found out he was about to lose his father and was still in shock. Jenny reasoned that there would be a more appropriate time to tell him about her experience. Once more she put off telling him as she had so many times before.

Jenny showered and put on a casual pair of trousers and a pretty top and cardigan. She applied a natural looking makeup that enhanced her dark eyes and wore her hair loose, thick waves framing her face. She put on the dainty silver necklace that Mike had bought her for their fifth wedding anniversary. She took a deep breath and went downstairs to face the day ahead.

It wasn't going to be easy...

Katie came bounding in with Barney, who was panting and dragging himself behind her. 'We went to the beach', she announced as she placed a handful of sand-covered shells and small pebbles that she'd collected onto the kitchen table. Barney went straight to his water bowl and began lapping, splashing water and drool over the flagstone floor.

'So I see', Jenny said glancing at the sandy mess on the table. 'Thank you for the note, by the way. Did you have a good time?'

'Yes it was lovely and we went to see Mary and the Reverend. She gave me lemonade and biscuits'. Katie was absorbed in sorting the pebbles from the pile. She had a vast collection lining shelves and the windowsill in her bedroom.

'That's nice of her', Jenny said, reaching for a dustpan and brush from the cupboard.

'Yes, she's always nice to me. She looked after me when I was little before'. Katie said.

'What do you mean, when you were little before? Before when?' Jenny asked absently as she swept up the sand from the table.

'Before I drowned in the cave, of course', Katie said bluntly, her attention on the pebbles.

Jenny stopped and looked aghast at her daughter. 'What are you talking about Katie? You've never drowned in a cave. You're telling stories again, aren't you?' Jenny was mildly irritated at Katie's remarks. She'd come out with all sorts of weird and wonderful things since she could talk but this was taking things a bit far. What with the painting of the house the other day and now this...

'*No*', Katie said indignantly. It was all the little girl could manage.

Jenny resumed her sweeping and let it go. She had enough to think about today.

Mike appeared in the kitchen and started to prepare breakfast for them all – cereal for Katie, fruit for Jenny and jam on toast for himself. It was the same routine every day. 'We were thinking of going to see Nan and Gramp today. What do you think, Katie?' Mike said cheerfully.

'*Yes!*' Katie shouted triumphantly, 'can we take Barney?'

Jenny could see the poor dog was exhausted after his walk on the beach. He was still panting and stretched flat out on the cool flagstones under the kitchen table. 'Perhaps we should leave him here today – look he's tired out, poor thing'.

'*Pleeeeese*', Katie chimed. She hated to be separated from the Doberman.

'We'll see but I think he needs a rest', Jenny said as she helped Mike with the breakfast. 'Come on, eat up and we'll get ready to go'. She placed a bowl of muesli and milk in front of Katie and she tucked in eagerly. Treacle parked himself next to her in the hope of falling scraps and Honey waddled into the kitchen, also aware of the daily breakfast routine.

They all ate breakfast in silence, scrutinised closely by the two Labradors. Mike was obviously trying hard to stay upbeat for Katie's sake but Jenny could see the haunting sadness in his eyes. She hoped there was something that could be done to prolong his father's life and keep him comfortable. He didn't deserve to suffer and had so many ambitions yet to be fulfilled. Life could be cruel sometimes, she thought.

'Mum, can we take Barney?' Katie was determined she wanted to take the Doberman.

Jenny looked at Barney, still resting under the table. He looked tired out. 'How about we take Honey instead? Treacle can stay here and keep Barney company – he hates it in the car anyway. Gramp can check Honey over and make sure the puppies are ok. What do you say?'

Katie looked over to Mike and he nodded his approval as he bit off a large piece of toast. 'Ok then', Katie readily agreed.

'I'll just text Dad and let him know we're coming', Mike said around a mouthful of toast.

Jenny fed the dogs and let them out into the garden. It was a fine day and fairly warm for early Autumn. The tide was coming in again and she loved the cycles of nature that she'd never even noticed living in London.

London. That jolted her memory. Bob had left another text message for her. It must have come through last evening but she'd ignored it with so much going on. She checked her phone in the kitchen. Yes, sure enough there was a silly message from Bob. 'This is getting a bit much now', Jenny said waving the phone in Mike's direction.

'Bob again is it?' Mike asked. She'd told him about her ex and how he'd been pestering her with silly messages.

'Yes and I'm getting pretty irritated now. I'll just ignore it. He'll give up eventually', Jenny said hopefully.

Mike rolled his eyes. He had enough on his plate. 'Come on then, are we all ready to go to Nan and Gramp's?'

Jenny and Katie shouted 'Yes' in unison and Jenny grabbed Honey's lead. The Labrador waddled to the door, her swollen abdomen swaying heavily from side to side.

'You stay and look after Barney', Jenny said to Treacle. The dog sat with his ball in his mouth looking dejected. 'Bye Barney', Jenny called out as she shut the front door after them all.

They piled into Mike's Range Rover and set off to visit his father, the atmosphere becoming tense as Jenny and Mike anticipated the emotional conversation. Katie sat behind them, humming to herself and stroking Honey's soft coat through the bars of the dog compartment in the back of the 4x4. Mike's parents lived ten miles away on the edge of an upmarket town. Their home was a restored period house with a large mature garden. Jenny loved the Victorian styling of the house and the way they had retained the antique feel of the place. She always felt welcome and at home there and had become a real part of their family when she and Mike had married. John and Martha had treated her like their own daughter. They also doted on Katie and were keen grandparents; although Jenny was reluctant to ask them to babysit Katie too often. It just didn't seem fair on them with their busy lives.

They travelled inland toward the town and soon they arrived at Mike's parent's house. A home he had been born and brought up in. They clambered out of the Range Rover, Mike carefully lifting Honey down – she was hesitating to jump from the car. As they walked up the path, Martha Halliday opened the heavy wooden front door to greet them. With hugs all round, she ushered them into the sitting room, as cheery as ever. Jenny knew she was an expert at covering up her feelings, especially for Katie's sake. Martha, as she always did, immediately went to make tea for everyone. Honey followed her into the kitchen.

Mike gave his father a manly hug along with a slap on the back. 'How are you doing Dad?' he asked.

'Oh I'm fine, son – don't worry about me', John said, returning the gesture.

Then it was Jenny's turn. Not knowing what to say, she hugged her father-in-law tightly, her gesture conveying her love and concern. She felt his strong arms envelop her. John Halliday was a giant of a man and rather rotund and cuddly. He reminded her of Father Christmas but without the beard. Always jolly, he laughed away her uneasiness.

'I'm fine, my dear', he whispered into her ear, trying to reassure her unspoken anxieties and knowing Mike had given her the bad news.

They settled down in the large sitting room, all avoided the mention of John's illness, acutely aware that Katie didn't know. John sat in his usual armchair and scooped his granddaughter into his arms, wincing briefly with pain but determined to sweep it aside.

'And how is my little cherub?' he said cheerily, 'and how is that old pooch of yours?' He was referring to Barney. He knew how strong the bond was between them.

'We went to the beach this morning', Katie said brightly.

'Well, that was good. You'll be back to school soon won't you? You'll miss those extra walks with him'. John was smiling at his little granddaughter, obviously aware that their time together was limited.

'Gramp, will you check Honey's puppies?' Katie asked.

John laughed. 'Yes of course I will. She must be due any day now'. Katie had insisted throughout Honey's pregnancy that he should be her obstetrician – just as he had looked after her and her mother. John had willingly gone along with it, although he'd admitted he was no vet.

Katie ran off to fetch Honey and returned with the Labrador waddling behind her. Martha followed bringing a tray of tea and home-made cakes. They all took their cups of tea and thanked Martha for baking such delicious cupcakes.

John called Honey over to him and she dutifully lay at his feet, knowing what was coming. With his enormous hands, he gently examined the dog's abdomen. 'Well, Katie, these little pups seem fine to me. Come and feel them move'.

Katie knelt beside the dog and her grandfather guided her tiny hand over one of the unborn puppies. They both waited, motionless with anticipation.

Suddenly, Katie's face lit up with amazement. 'It moved. I can feel the puppy move.' The little girl was enthralled.

Jenny watched, her heart melting with joy and pride at her family. She knew Katie would take the news of her grandfather's illness extremely hard and vowed to allow them both a little more time and happiness together before it became necessary to tell her and break the magical bond of love they shared.

It would be heart-breaking.

Martha drained her china teacup and as astute as ever, she encouraged Katie to join her with Honey in the garden. She was well aware that John, Mike and Jenny needed to talk.

Jenny could see Katie through the window. Martha was pushing her on the swing they had installed for her on the old beech tree. Honey was sniffing among the immaculately kept flower beds. It was a picture of normality, yet this day was anything but normal.

Mike became serious. 'Dad, I'd like to have a chat with your oncologist. Maybe there's a chance we could operate'.

'Son, I don't think that's going to make a scrap of difference. I've already been through all the options with them and they're certain the tumour is inoperable. We just have to accept it now'. John seemed resigned to his fate.

Mike started to protest but his father cut in. 'Mike, I understand what you're trying to do but the tumour is just too big. The chemo didn't touch it, even with the FU2. All they can do is offer palliative care. Surgery is out of the question'.

'What about radiotherapy then?' Mike asked.

'It's a possibility to relieve symptoms but it's not curable. To be honest, I don't want to go through all that. You're a doctor – you know what it entails and I don't want to end my days trying one thing after another. Just let nature take its course'. John had obviously thought through his options and resolutely made up his mind.

Mike smoothed his fingers through his hair, lost for words.

John could see his distress. 'I know it's hard to accept but your mother and I have discussed it. We just have to make the most of the time I have left'.

Jenny watched as father and son tried to reconcile themselves with what had happened. John's diagnosis had come out of the blue. If he'd been ill lately, he'd covered it up well. Jenny understood why he'd resisted telling them – he was protecting his family as her and Mike had with Katie. She wondered how she could help.

'Dad, have you arranged some nursing care? What about pain relief? You have to make sure you have that under control'. Jenny was ready to step in and look after her father-in-law whenever he needed her.

John turned to Jenny. 'I don't want to go into that hospice of yours', he was adamant. 'I want to die at home'. His face was set with determination, his big hands gripping the arms of the chair as if he was going to be dragged away. Suddenly he looked frightened and vulnerable for the first time.

Jenny's eyes were moist with tears. She loved him like she did her own father and she'd do anything to grant him his dying wishes. She ran over to him and crouched beside him, taking his hand tightly in both of hers. 'Dad, I will always be here for you. I'll give up work and look after you at home when the time comes – you never have to worry about that. Mum will be here too and Mike'.

John patted her shoulder with his free hand. 'I know you will, sweetheart, I know'. His voice was breaking with emotion.

Jenny looked over at Mike. He nodded his agreement but was deep in thought. His face was twisted with worry. It was heart wrenching for Jenny to see him so distressed and forlorn.

Suddenly there was a tap on the window. Jenny turned to see Katie outside beckoning to her mother to join her in the garden. 'I'd better see what she wants', Jenny said. She kissed John's cheek as she stood to leave. 'It will be ok, Dad, you'll see'.

John nodded quietly as she went through the kitchen and into the garden. Jenny would tell John about her near death experience some day. She knew it would help him cope with the uncertainty of death and the terrifying thought that there was nothing beyond this life. John deserved to die in peace with the reassurance that his consciousness – his spirit – would live on in the most blissful place imaginable. He deserved to know about the love and acceptance that awaited him.

'Mum, come and play with us', Katie was urging her to join her and her grandmother in a game of hide and seek. Honey had wandered off to explore the pond at the bottom of the garden.

Jenny had never felt less like playing but she couldn't show Katie there was anything wrong and she felt that she owed her daughter at least some time together after spending most of her school holidays at work. Jenny glanced over at Martha. Her mother-in-law smiled a benevolent smile. Unspoken words of empathy exchanged between the two women. Martha understood precisely how Jenny felt. She had lost her mother-in-law to a stroke and had nursed her at home, years before. She'd also been a working mother herself during her career. She'd been a paediatrician all through Mike's childhood, although she'd retired in her late fifties to enjoy her garden and take care of her family. Jenny felt a close bond with Martha and knew that despite the strong persona she displayed to the world, she loved her husband and her family dearly and would be crushed at the prospect of losing John. Jenny's heart went out to her.

Katie was getting agitated and eager to start their game. 'OK, I'll count and you two hide', Jenny said, placing her palms over her eyes. 'One, two, three, four...' She heard them scurrying off to hide.

Finally, Jenny reached one hundred. 'Coming, ready or not', she shouted as she began to hunt for them. There was no sign of Katie or Martha.

Jenny glanced across at the sitting room window, wondering how Mike and his father were getting on. She was puzzled to see what appeared to be an animated argument going on between the two men. Mike looked like he was imploring his father to agree with him over something, but John was shaking his head and gesturing that he didn't want any part of it. Jenny briefly looked behind a large rhododendron bush – there was still no sign of Katie or Martha. She was intrigued to see how the argument would progress between Mike and John and manoeuvred herself so she could see the men more clearly through the window, still pretending to be seeking Katie.

As she continued to watch, it looked like Mike was becoming exasperated with his father. He was obviously pushing to make a point but John was resisting. Then, in a heart-warming moment, Jenny watched as John gestured that he'd given in and lost the argument and the two men fell into one another's arms, both overtaken by emotion. She couldn't tell what that had been all about but she was glad that it ended amicably.

Jenny crept around a delicately scented rose bed and called playfully to Katie. 'Where are you? I must be getting close'. There was no answer.

Then Katie jumped out from behind a dense shrub and shrieked with delight. Martha also came out from her hiding place behind the potting shed. They all laughed in a moment of light relief for the women as Katie skipped across to stroke Honey, who was lying full out on the lawn near the pond.

Jenny affectionately touched Martha on the arm. 'How are you coping, Mum?' she asked.

Martha shrugged. 'It's a shock but I'm getting used to it slowly. He's been in pain for months before his diagnosis but wouldn't go and see about it. He can be downright stubborn sometimes'. Martha seemed angry and upset that her husband had left it so long to seek medical help.

Jenny knew this was a normal reaction. Martha was going through the process that would eventually lead to her acceptance of her husband's inexorable death. She wished she could make it easier for her.

'Perhaps he was too frightened to get a diagnosis. As a doctor, he probably knows too much', Jenny offered.

'I expect he was but if it could have been caught early, surgery would have been an option and we might not be faced with losing him now'. Martha shook her head is dismay.
Jenny turned to see Mike striding toward them. 'I have to go into the hospital', he said apologetically.

Jenny was disappointed. They hadn't spent a clear day together for weeks and he was needed here to support his parents. 'What is it, an emergency?' Jenny asked.

'Something like that', Mike said as he kissed Jenny and then his mother. 'Sorry, I'll be back as soon as I can'. With that he was gone.

Jenny sighed. This was the part of their life she hated. It was a rare thing for her to be able to rely on Mike to be available when he was so often on call but lately, he seemed to be constantly at work or dashing off somewhere, even on scheduled days off. She knew he had extra responsibilities as acting general surgical consultant and he was ambitious to develop his career. She had to live with it, like it or not...

'Never mind', Martha said. 'Let's have another game of hide and seek'.

It was Katie's turn to count while Jenny and Martha hid. For the next hour, they played happily in the garden while John sat on his garden bench watching, Honey lying at his feet. The weather was idyllic. Not too warm but with clear blue skies. For a short time, it was as if the tragic news of John's cancer was just an unpleasant dream. There was no sign from John that he'd argued with his son. Whatever it had been about appeared to be forgotten or at least brushed under the carpet and Jenny let it go.

Eventually, Mike returned and they all had a late lunch together – a casserole that Martha had prepared earlier that morning. Mike didn't mention what the emergency was and neither Jenny nor his parents asked. He seemed in a brighter mood and Jenny wanted to enjoy the family atmosphere in the house and avoid the subject of work.

By late afternoon, the sun was low in the sky and it was time to get Katie and Honey home. Barney and Treacle would be ready for their walk and Jenny was looking forward to a relaxing evening alone with Mike. They needed some quiet time together after all that had happened.

They said their goodbyes with hugs all round and a fuss for Honey. Mike lifted the pregnant Labrador into the back of the Range Rover and they set off for home.

'Bye Katie', Martha called as Mike drove off.

Soon they were on the coast road that led back to the cottage. They travelled in silence, each caught up with their own memories of the day.

'Look at this bloody idiot', Mike said abruptly as he saw a Land Rover lurching toward them. It was swerving wildly across the road. 'He looks drunk'.

Jenny could see it was the Reverend Wheelan's car and she had to agree – it looked like the driver was drunk and veering out of control.

As the two vehicles came closer, Mike was forced off the road and into the hedge to avoid the Land Rover hitting them full on. Mike slammed his hand down on the horn, blasting obscenities and watching the Land Rover in his rear-view mirror as it disappeared down the road.

Jenny was shocked as she and Katie were thrown against the side of the car, Honey scrabbling to stay upright in the back. Katie screamed and Jenny tried to reassure her, the immediate danger apparently over. Nobody was hurt but Mike was clearly angry with the driver. He crunched the gearstick into first, pushed hard on the accelerator and the Range Rover pulled out of the hedge and back onto the road, the back wheels kicking up mud from the verge.

'He could have got us killed, the mad bastard', Mike said through gritted teeth.

Jenny stayed silent. She'd seen the look on Wheelan's face as he careered toward them. She sensed the wild hatred in his eyes and the very blackness in his soul for a brief moment.

A feeling of impending doom washed over her as somewhere deep in her psyche she recognised he was capable of a dark and malevolent brutality.

She felt an icy shiver cascading down her spine…

There was something about him she'd always found disturbingly creepy and after this, there was no way she would allow Katie to visit him ever again.

Chapter five: a deadly secret

Wheelan peered at his reflection in the hall mirror. He looked a complete mess. His eyes were bloodshot and the whites were starting to turn an alarming brownish-orange colour. His skin was pale and he was losing weight. It was no wonder if Mary *had* been poisoning him, he thought. More than ever he believed she'd be capable of something like that.

The scar on his cheek seemed ever more prominent as he got older. It was a constant reminder that he'd murdered Helen. He brushed his fingers over the scar. If only she had loved him back, he thought. None of this with Mary or Morgan would have happened. His life might have gone in a completely different direction. Maybe they would have had little Kate and they would have been a happy family together. Instead of that, he'd lost his temper and killed someone he professed to love. He'd been besotted with her yet she barely knew he existed. It was always Morgan she'd been after.

Wheelan sighed. That was over thirty years ago. Why did he keep churning it over and over in his mind? He had more urgent things to worry about at the moment. Like the fact that Mary had him in a pincer movement. She knew about his criminal drug dealing and was intending to put that knowledge to good use to get what she wanted. And she could be very determined when she wanted to be.

Wheelan had been up worrying half the night. He'd taken a few more whiskeys but his stomach pain had become much worse and he felt too nauseous to swallow anything except antacid tablets. Now, after a restless night's sleep, he was fretting again because Mary was due soon and he wasn't sure what was in store for him. He wished he could just escape somewhere away from it all. Typical, he thought – just when I've spent all the money on buying this place, I want to get away from it. If only he'd known all this a few days ago. He could be on a beach in the Bahamas now...

Wheelan looked out of the small window in the hallway to see Mary's car turning the corner toward the chapel. Bloody hell, here we go, he thought. She's keen today, she's an hour early. What's she playing at? He watched as the car drew up outside the door.

Wheelan scooted into the sitting room, instinctively trying to avoid her. He immersed himself in yesterday's newspaper, pretending to read.

'Good morning, Lucas'. Mary called cheerfully.

We're back to first names now are we, he thought, not sure if that was a good sign or not.

Mary hung her coat on the coat rack in the hall and strode confidently into the sitting room, her chunky frame filling the doorway as she headed toward the Reverend. She plonked herself down on the footstool in front of him, revealing a voluptuous cleavage that was threatening to spill out of her top. This was something she'd never normally do. This looked ominous, Wheelan thought. He put the paper down and she had his full attention.

'Now Lucas, I've been thinking since our little chat last night'. Mary stopped to push her hair back from her chubby face, her lips bright red with fresh lipstick.

Oh dear, what's coming next, Wheelan's stomach knotted painfully. This didn't feel right at all.

'I think it's high time I moved in here and looked after you properly. You're looking very thin and you're drinking far too much. You need looking after', Mary's voice was bright and cheerful as if nothing had happened.

Wheelan's jaw dropped with the shock of her audacious revelation. There was absolutely no way he'd let that happen. No way in this world or the next.

Mary went on before he could gather his senses. 'You know it makes sense, my dear. There's no point in both of us having separate houses. We're not getting any younger you know. We can live together and save money for nice holidays and treats'. She smiled brightly at him, her hand reaching out to grab his.

Wheelan deftly moved his hand and shuffled back in his chair in an attempt to avoid her. Good God – what the hell was all this? Mary had taken him by surprise, no doubt about that, but surely he could fend her off? He had to.

'I could put my house on the market later today. What do you think?'

Mary didn't wait for a reply. Before he could think of a response, she leaned toward him and kissed him full on the mouth, her wet sticky lips smacking noisily against his. She stood and strode out to the kitchen like she already owned the place.

Wheelan was stunned. He reached for the handkerchief in his pocket and rubbed feverishly at his mouth, wiping away streaks of gooey lipstick and saliva. He shuddered. This was way too much. It was outrageous.

Wheelan heard Mary clattering about in the kitchen as usual. He had to stop this wretched nonsense. Over his dead body would she move in with him and she could stop this blatant over-familiarity as well. He wiped his mouth again with the back of his hand. What the hell was it coming to?

He sat for several minutes, wondering how best to handle the situation. She obviously thought she had one over on him with her insight into his drug dealing but he didn't honestly think she'd turn him in and see him rot in jail. She might be conniving but she wasn't a villain like Morgan. It was all his doing, the bastard. He'd roped her in so he could ramp up the blackmail if it became necessary. Wheelan realised that because he had been so weak and compliant, Morgan had never needed to reveal his and Mary's secret arrangement. Now Morgan was dead, Mary was taking up the rains and had seized her opportunity to get her own way. And he'd played right into her hands...

Well, he wasn't having any of it. He'd have to nip this in the bud right now.

Wheelan stood and straightened his sweater. He ran his fingers through his hair as if he meant business. He took a deep breath and walked through to the kitchen. Mary was peeling potatoes and humming tunelessly, a self-righteous smirk on her face.

Wheelan coughed. 'Mary, you can't move in. There's no way you can do that, so don't even think about it'. He had one hand on his hip, the other steadying himself against the kitchen table. He hoped he'd sounded authoritative enough to make her realise he meant it.

'You know it makes perfect sense, Lucas. We're both alone now and it will be lovely for us both to have company'. Mary hardly looked up from the potatoes but she was obviously serious about moving in by the tone of her voice.

Wheelan dug his heels in. 'No Mary, I'm not having it'.

'Don't you remember our little chat last night? I know all about your dirty little secrets'. Mary glanced at him triumphantly.

Wheelan called her bluff. If she cared about him as she said she did, then she would never carry out her threat. She was simply using her knowledge as leverage to get what she wanted. But if he couldn't put her off, his life would be hell.

'Do what you like. You're not moving in here and I'll do whatever I have to do to stop you'. Wheelan felt confident now. He wasn't about to let any woman control him.

Abruptly, Mary slammed the potatoes and the peeling knife onto the kitchen counter and spun round to face him. She had raw anger in her eyes. 'Do you realise how easily I could have you arrested and put behind bars?' Mary stood glaring at him, waiting for an answer.

'You wouldn't do that. Not after all we've been through over the years'. Wheelan was taken aback and trying to appeal to her on an emotional level but it wasn't working.

'I've got far more on you than just your petty drug dealing'. Mary said spitefully.

Wheelan felt a crashing wave of panic. Did she know about the youth he'd killed the other day? Had Morgan told her about Helen's murder? This sounded serious...

'Oh yeah – what do you mean by that?' Wheelan tried not to let his voice shake.

'Come on Lucas. What about the bodies?'

Wheelan felt sick again.

She knew he was a killer!

He'd tried so hard all these years to keep the awful truth from her but she'd known all along. Damn that bastard Morgan. He'd definitely kill him now if he wasn't already dead. He felt renewed anger for the man that had overshadowed his life for so long. Why did he have to tell Mary that he'd killed Helen? He'd sworn he would never tell a soul.

Wheelan's mouth gaped open uselessly. He was lost for words.

'You must have known Terry had killed those boys?' Mary said.

'What boys?' Wheelan was puzzled. This was the first he'd heard of it.

'Those drug addicts. He stabbed the two of them. You must have known'.

Wheelan was still gob struck. He really hadn't heard about any of this.

'Anyway', Mary said, 'I can pin the murders on you quite easily'. She said it in a very matter of fact way as if she already had it all worked out.

She'd obviously been watching too many murder mysteries to come out with something like that. This wasn't the Mary he knew. What the hell was she doing? Wheelan knew Morgan hadn't killed anyone. He would have bragged endlessly about it if he had. This was a bit extreme if she was trying to get him to agree to her moving in.

Wheelan almost laughed. 'This is ridiculous, Mary. You're making it up'. He turned to go; not wanting to listen to any more. She obviously didn't know about Helen or the lout he killed the other day or she'd have used that against him, not this ludicrous nonsense.

'I'm not making it up and I can prove it to you'. Mary said firmly.

'Really! How? Are you going to take me to see the bodies?' Wheelan laughed again. It was a hollow laugh.

'OK then, yes, if that's what it takes'. Mary stood her ground and glared defiantly at him.

Wheelan couldn't believe how this conversation was going. Would Mary stop at nothing to have her way with him? It was all bluff he was sure, but he decided to go along with it. It would be fun to see her squirm when things turned around and he got the upper hand.

'OK then, show me'. Wheelan gestured to her to lead the way.

Mary nodded, still defiant. She fished for something in her bag, pushing it into the pocket of her trousers. Then she grabbed a large torch which Wheelan kept on the kitchen windowsill before she made her way out from the back door of the manse. Wheelan dutifully followed. They walked in silence as she led him up into the woods, a litter of fallen leaves beginning to gather on the narrow path.

They must have walked for a quarter of a mile uphill through thick undergrowth and into the deciduous ancient woodland beyond, climbing over a fence and pushing through dense vegetation as they went.

Finally, Mary stopped. Her face was gleaming with perspiration and her breathing was laboured. 'Ready for this?' She said smugly.

Wheelan nodded wearily. He too was out of breath from the walk and his stomach was burning with pain. He was still not convinced she had anything to show him. He hoped it wasn't a ploy for her to get sloppy with him again. He couldn't bare that twice in one day.

Mary turned and beat her way through the undergrowth with a fallen branch she'd found. She stopped when she reached some old stones at the side of the hill. Wheelan couldn't quite see what lay beyond; the vegetation was thick with bushes, brambles and tree saplings. Mary pulled a large iron key from her pocket and Wheelan heard her unlock a door.

'Come on then', she urged him.

Wheelan followed her through a heavy wooden door and into a dark tunnel that had been excavated into the hill. She flicked the torch on. Their shadows loomed menacingly around the stone walls of the tunnel as Mary led him further into the cloying darkness. Old cobwebs caught in their hair and clothes and Wheelan could hear their footsteps echoing all around them. The tunnel was cold and damp. He shivered, hoping there wouldn't be rats in there. God how he hated rats...

Wheelan was stunned. He never knew this place existed. 'Where are we?' he asked.

'This is one of the secret caverns that belong to the ruined castle up ahead', Mary said. 'The other entrance was bricked up years ago and this was left to crumble away. But as you can see it survived'.

They moved further into the cavern, the low ceiling and narrow walls now opening out into a dark cavernous vault. Away from the fresh air outside, the place reeked. It stank of putrid rotting flesh and rat droppings and water seeped through the old stone walls. Wheelan tried not to touch anything, glancing round anxiously looking for rodents. He thought he saw something small move in the shadows.

Mary stopped and turned to him. 'Here we are', she said. 'Here's your evidence'.

She ceremoniously turned the flashlight onto a tangled mound of bones and decomposing human remains in the corner of the cavern.

'That's Terry's handiwork, but who would ever know that it wasn't you? All it would take is a phone call…' Mary said victoriously.

Wheelan was dumbfounded.

How the bloody hell was he going to get out of this?

Chapter six: tempers rising

Mike's angry outburst at the drunken Reverend seemed to set the mood for the next few days. Mike had gradually become more aloof and preoccupied and Jenny felt decidedly uneasy about it. There was something going on with him but when she tried to talk about it, he just snapped back at her. After days of crossed words, she thought it best to leave him alone – it was understandable that he was in an emotional turmoil as he struggled to accept his father's inevitable death. She would just have to be more understanding and patient with him. Anyway, she had enough to contend with trying to look after Katie and getting her ready for a new school term. It was coming up fast and she had school uniforms, shoes and other things to shop for before the end of the week if they were to be ready in time. She was also booked in for more shifts at the hospital and later that day, she had a late shift on Mike's surgical ward. She hoped he'd be in a better mood.

Katie had been busy painting pictures over the past couple of days but eventually, after some gentle nagging from Jenny, she'd agreed to tidy her room. Now she'd come downstairs with a bag of unwanted toys to donate to the charity shop. 'Here you are, Mum, you can have these but I'm not getting rid of my big teddy'. Katie left the bag in the hallway.

'Good girl, Katie, all finished and ready to pass inspection?' Jenny asked, pleased that she'd finally tidied up the mess in her bedroom. Fair play to her, Jenny thought, she usually did a good job of it once she got around to tackling the task.

'Yes, all finished', Katie said. 'Can I take Barney for a walk now?'

Jenny was wary of letting her go to the beach alone. She knew she liked to visit the Reverend and his housekeeper but after the episode the other day, she didn't want Katie anywhere near that drunken maniac. If she could put her off for a few more days, Katie would be back in school and she would have fewer opportunities to go to the beach or the manse. Jenny looked at Katie and could see she was desperate to go out. How could she refuse such a delightful little girl a walk on the beach? She looked at the clock – she had just enough time to go with her before Laura arrived and she had to leave for her shift at the hospital. She could distract Katie from visiting the manse without making an issue of it.

'OK then – I'll come with you but it will have to be a quick one before I go to work', Jenny said. She could see Katie nodding excitedly in agreement, especially as that meant they would take the other dogs too.

Jenny grabbed three leads and Treacle fetched his ball and bounded over to the front door ready to go out. Barney scrambled awkwardly to his feet, his old joints clicking and stiff. Honey finally roused herself from her basket, keen to join them despite being uncomfortable with her advancing pregnancy.

'Come on Honey, a walk will do you good', Jenny said, sympathetically.

They all left the house and headed toward the slipway to the beach. It was another fine day but there was a stiff breeze coming in from the sea and fluffy cumulus clouds obscured the sun intermittently as they drifted across the sky. The sea was choppy and the tide was halfway up the beach but there was still plenty of sand for the dogs to play. Katie skipped along next to her mother and Treacle ran off ahead, eager to take in all the new smells, his ball, as ever, jammed into his mouth. Barney and Honey plodded slowly behind but seemed happy to be out in the bracing sea air.

They passed the spot where Jenny had collapsed and almost died over nine years ago. She couldn't help but think of it every time they went past. She looked at her beautiful daughter and at Barney and was glad she'd come back to this life. She remembered how her beloved Doberman had been snatched by Bob and recalled the strange spectre of seeing him being driven away while she was hovering several feet above her body. Since her brush with death, Barney seemed even more precious to her. She was glad Bob had seen sense and brought him back – life without Barney was unthinkable...

'Look, Mum, a raven', Katie pointed to the sky.

Jenny looked up and sure enough a large black raven swooped down over the cliff top. 'So it is. Well spotted Katie'. Jenny felt proud of her daughter. She was bright and interested in the world around her. She felt sure she would be successful in life, whatever career she pursued. Katie was her reason for living. Had she died that day, she'd never have had the amazing experience of being a mother and the pleasure of having such a wonderful family. Yes, she was glad she'd come back, although there were days when she remembered her experience with great nostalgia. It had been more intense and beautiful than anything on Earth. She hoped things between her and Mike would improve soon. She hated feeling so disconnected from him.

As they neared the bottom of the slipway to the beach, Jenny noticed the Reverend's Land Rover and Mary's red Fiat outside the manse. She felt an inexplicable feeling of apprehension as she passed the chapel and her stomach was knotted and tense. In the first few months after her near death experience, she liked to go to the Sunday services on occasions – not because she was religious, but because somehow the Reverend intrigued her.

But there was always something nagging at the back of her mind about him. It was an elusive feeling. She felt a strange connection to him, but couldn't explain it. As time went by, she had gone to the chapel less and less. She liked to sit there alone sometimes during the week when it was quiet but it made her feel sad and lonely. Somehow, she felt an intense sense of loss just being there in that building and since Katie was born, she'd stopped going completely. She'd begun to feel a growing resistance to the place – as if something would happen if she went there. Logically, it was totally unreasonable but her heightened intuition warned her to stay away.

She wished Katie would too but since her daughter had grown and been allowed the freedom to go to the beach with Barney, she had taken to visiting the manse. Jenny didn't approve and she knew that Katie often visited without telling her. She wished she wouldn't do it but how could she explain to a seven year old that her mother had a gut feeling there was something bad about the Reverend – supposedly a man of God? She had no evidence whatsoever and as much as she loved her daughter, Katie could be wilful at times. She had a streak of rebellion in her and if Jenny insisted she mustn't go it would make Katie even more determined.

'Throw the ball for Treacle, Mum', Katie was asking. 'You can throw it further than me'.

They had walked down to the water's edge and the tide was coming in fast now. 'OK', Jenny laughed and took the ball from Katie. She threw it into the sea and Treacle eagerly chased after it, splashing through the waves.

They spent the next forty minutes enjoying their fun on the beach with the dogs. Barney and Honey preferred to move at a more leisurely pace but Treacle raced around the beach chasing his ball and running with Katie. They reluctantly started headed for home so Jenny could get off to her shift at the hospital and they began the steep climb back to the cottage.

Laura had arrived by the time they got home and Jenny quickly changed and handed over to the babysitter, barely getting out of the cottage on time.

'Oh sweetheart, I'll miss you', Jenny told Katie as she kissed her goodbye. She would much rather have stayed home, especially as Mike had been so distant with her lately. She wanted more than anything to call the ward and say she wouldn't be in but her conscience wouldn't let her. She knew she was needed at work and it was too late to find a replacement nurse from the agency. Resolutely, she got into the Citroen.

'See you later,' Jenny shouted as she drove off. Katie was waving madly after her, Barney at her side in the doorway. Jenny felt the familiar wrench of leaving Katie to go to work. She briefly wondered if she should just give it all up and stay home. Then she remembered some of her patients and how she loved being a nurse too – it was far more than just earning a living, although they depended on both her and Mike's salary. It was a dilemma with no easy answer. Once Katie was back in school, Jenny knew she'd feel a little better about being out at work but she hated having to leave her with someone else, even though Laura was the perfect babysitter in so many ways.

Jenny sighed as she left her car in the hospital car park and made her way to the surgical ward. She greeted people she knew as she walked through the corridor, the hum of activity and the familiarity of the building giving her a different sense of belonging. Her identity since her early twenties had hinged around being a nurse – it was all she knew and it would be hard to relinquish. Somehow she had to find a way to juggle her career and her family.

Jenny Changed into blue scrubs and started her shift. Mike was nowhere to be seen but she knew he would be on the ward at some point later in the day.

'Your hubbie is in theatre this afternoon, Jenny', Jenny's colleague said after she'd finished handing over her patients. 'He's got a pretty big list today'.

'Thanks Sue, I'm bound to catch up with him later. I'll make a start on the medicine round', Jenny said. She was secretly glad Mike wasn't around. The way he'd snubbed her lately had felt uncomfortable. She hated confrontation of any kind and had suffered it in silence – as usual. If she could only focus on her work and Katie, perhaps he'd come around in his own time. He was still dealing with the news about his father after all and it wasn't like him to be moody. He was usually so happy and cheerful and so loving. Jenny wished things could get back to normal.

She found the keys to the medicine trolley and began her rounds, assisted by one of the junior nurses. The ward was full to capacity with thirty general surgical patients, both pre- and post-operative cases. Nursing staff were thin on the ground due to an outbreak of gastroenteritis among the staff. Jenny, as a senior staff nurse, had to administer medicines to all the patients. Many of the post-operative patients were taking controlled drugs such as morphine to relieve their pain and that meant careful counting and record keeping. It would take the best part of an hour.

As she worked her way from one patient to the next, she noticed that most of them had been prescribed a new antibiotic, bravafloxacin. The drug had only come on to the market during the past two months. Mike's signature was on the drug chart. It was unusual for so many patients to be prescribed antibiotics – especially the exact same drug. Perhaps he'd ordered them prophylactically as a precaution against the virulent stomach bug. That would also explain why both pre- and post-operative patients were on the drug. Antibiotics only tended to be prescribed as needed for conditions such as post-operative wound infections or chest infections – not for almost everybody like this.

'Here's your medication, Mr Evans', Jenny said as she handed a small plastic medicine cup to her patient containing ibuprofen 400mg for post-operative pain relief and 100mg dose of bravafloxacin.

'Thanks nurse but I'm feeling sick and having palpitations – I'm sure it's the antibiotics', Mr Evans said rubbing his chest as if to emphasise the point.

'OK, I'll have a word with the doctor when he comes up to the ward', Jenny said with a reassuring touch to his arm. She straightened his bed sheets and plumped his pillows.

The next patient had overheard their conversation and also complained of nausea and itchy skin. He refused to take the antibiotic.

Jenny moved on to the next patient and sure enough bravafloxacin was prescribed on the drug sheet along with the ibuprofen analgesia.

'How are you feeling, Mr Williams?' Jenny asked as she handed him his medication and poured him a fresh glass of water.

'Not too bad thank you nurse. The pain from my wound is easing off but I am feeling really sick and light-headed', he said, reaching for a tissue.

'When did you start feeling sick?' Jenny asked.

'About two days ago, and it's getting much worse today', the patient answered.

Jenny checked his drug sheet. He was prescribed bravafloxacin two days ago and had taken eight doses so far. His symptoms could certainly be caused by the side-effects of the antibiotic, she thought. She double checked with some of the other patients that had complained of nausea and all of them had started the antibiotic exactly two days ago. This was strange, she thought. What was Mike playing at? This was not usual procedure. She would have to ask him about it later.

Jenny finally completed the medicine round and securely locked her drug trolley. 'Thanks for your help, Amy. Will you change Mr Williams' dressing for me please?' she asked the junior nurse. The girl nodded and scurried off.

Jenny spent the next few hours busily caring for her patients. One woman had vomited over the bed and needed changing. Another patient's wound had burst a couple of sutures and needed butterfly strips to hold the wound together and Mr Evans' palpitations had become so severe, that Jenny had to hook him up to a heart monitor and record an ECG. There were also three more patients to prepare for theatre. They were having elective surgery for minor conditions – the first, a hernia; another, an appendectomy and the third, a haemorrhoidectomy. The first patient on the afternoon list was already in the operating room and Mike was performing a major bowel resection. He would probably come up to the ward after that and leave the minor surgery to the registrar.

There was a buzz of activity on the ward, with nurses and doctors scurrying about their work. Hospital porters were taking patients back and forth to other departments; cleaners were mopping and dusting the ward. Heart monitors were bleeping and phones were ringing constantly. There was the all-pervading smell of hospital antiseptic. It was frenzied but Jenny loved the pandemonium and thrived on the atmosphere of a busy ward. It had been her life and she couldn't imagine any other career.

Just as they got on top of the work and the ward began to quieten down, Mike's bowel resection patient arrived back on the ward. He was still sleepy from the anaesthetic and Jenny helped to transfer him from the trolley to his bed. She organised the tangle of intravenous tubes, wound drainage bags and the man's new colostomy bag. It would be a difficult transition for him to adjust to, Jenny thought. She settled him comfortably into bed and checked his wound. It looked clean and dry. Then she flipped through his observation charts with recordings of the man's blood pressure, temperature and heart rate along with a fluid balance chart and his drug chart. Once again, Jenny noted that Mike had prescribed bravafloxacin. The first few doses were to be given via intravenous injection, and then he was to start on the 100mg capsules when he was eating again. This was really unusual, Jenny thought. There was no clinical indication that the man should be given antibiotics.

Mike finally arrived on the ward to check his patient, still in blue scrubs from the operating theatre. He had a stethoscope slung around his neck. He was fit and tanned and strode through the ward with an air of authority that came from natural charisma rather than a blatant wielding of his power. Since becoming acting consultant, while Mr Westland was on a sabbatical, he'd risen to the challenge admirably and would make an excellent consultant surgeon. Jenny still felt that rush of love and admiration for Mike that she'd felt when they first met, although she hoped his mood was less intense than it had been of late.

Jenny finished attaching a collection bag to the patient's catheter tube. She washed her hands and strode across the ward toward Mike. He was leaning on the nurse's station studying the patient's notes. 'Hi there', Jenny said, smiling brightly.

Mike looked up and smiled back at his wife. 'Hi Jenny, how are you? You're having a busy day by the look of it.' He nodded in the direction of the apparent mayhem on the ward.

'It's been really busy but it's starting to quieten down. How did your theatre list go – all finished?' She said.

'Yeah, all done. I just have to review a couple of patient's then I can take a break. How's my little Katie?'

He did seem chattier this afternoon, Jenny thought. Perhaps his mood was finally lifting. 'She's as gorgeous as ever', Jenny smiled at the thought of their daughter. 'We took the dogs to the beach this morning – it was great to get some fresh air and exercise. I think it was good for Honey to get out too'.

'That's nice. I'm looking forward to getting home, Mike said, returning his attention to the notes.

Jenny nodded in agreement. 'By the way, Mike, I noticed you've prescribed bravafloxacin to a lot of the patients on the ward. Is there any reason for it that we should be aware of?' Jenny asked, remembering the drug charts.

Mike looked up from the notes again. He struggled for a moment to find an answer. 'I don't want to take any chances with this gastroenteritis. If the patients get it, it will spread like wildfire. It's just a precaution'. He half smiled at Jenny and started to move away.

'OK, that's fine but some of them could be having side effects – mainly nausea and itchy skin. And Mr Evans has had pretty severe palpitations. I've recorded an ECG for you to look at'. Jenny sensed that Mike was beginning to get irritated.

He briefly glanced back at her as he walked away, 'I'm sure they'll be fine, it's not unusual'. He waived away her concerns and went to find his patient.

Jenny sighed. She thought Mike was getting over the moodiness but it was still there lurking under the surface. She could ask one of the junior doctors about it but since Mike had prescribed the medication, it ought to be him that dealt with it. She would try again before he left the ward for the day.

Jenny was called by one of the junior nurses to double check a patient's wound and then she had to take some test results over the phone. Another nurse called in sick with diarrhoea and vomiting and she had to arrange cover through the agency. Before she knew it, Mike was about to leave for home and she still hadn't been able to get him to look at the patient's prescriptions and the possible side-effects of the new antibiotic.

She cut her phone call short and hurried after him as he left the ward, making for the doctor's changing room. She called after him.

It was then she saw Bob walking purposefully down the corridor toward them.

Jenny's heart sank. What the hell was he doing here? She had enough to contend with without this.

Mike had seen him before she had and was now striding toward her ex-husband. Jenny could sense the tension between the two men as she hurried to catch up to them.

She couldn't hear what was being said but they were having a very heated exchange.

Suddenly Mike swung his arm back and punched Bob square in the face before he walked away, rubbing his fist.

Bob slumped against the wall, shocked at the doctor's sudden outburst. His nose was broken and bright red blood was dripping down his shirt.

Jenny quickly caught up and approached Bob. 'What the hell are you doing here?' She hissed the words at him, angry that he'd refused to leave her alone.

Bob mumbled through a blood-soaked handkerchief he had pressed against his nose. 'Sorry, I was down here anyway and wanted to see you'.

Jenny felt exasperated. Her relationship with Bob had been over for years yet he still wouldn't let it go. 'Why do you have to spoil everything for me Bob? Please, for pity's sake, just leave me alone!'

She was crying with frustration as she went off to find her husband.

Chapter seven: a crisis of conscience

The stench in the cavern was utterly repulsive and Wheelan couldn't wait to get out of there. He'd seen enough. Mary wanted to linger, wallowing in her renewed sense of power but Wheelan turned and made his way toward the shaft of daylight from the entrance. Mary followed close behind.

Wheelan blinked in the bright sunshine as his eyes adjusted to daylight. Mary followed seconds later and she locked the wooden door behind them. She put the key back in her pocket. They retraced their steps down the hill toward the manse in silence.

Wheelan knew Mary still had the upper hand. She was enjoying every minute of it. How could he have been so blind, so stupid? He felt utterly betrayed.

'What happened?' Wheelan finally asked.

'Terry killed those lads years ago. They were layabout drug addicts and they were threatening him so he stabbed them. He brought their bodies here and as far as I know, nobody even realised they were missing. There were no police, no newspapers – nothing'. Mary turned to look at Wheelan, remorse now in her eyes.

Was she sorry she'd turned on him like this? Did she regret spoiling their friendship with her startling revelations? Wheelan knew things would never be the same. Mary was tough and determined. It was looking more and more like she'd do whatever it took to get her way.

Wheelan was still shocked. Why hadn't Morgan mentioned the fact that he'd stabbed two young men and hidden their bodies? Was Mary in on that too? He had to know.

'How did you know they were there? Were you in on it?

'Goodness no!' Mary said. 'Terry told me just a few months before he died. He brought me here to show me the evidence. He intended to frame you if you didn't comply with his drug dealing plan. I didn't believe it either at first. I was ill for days after. It really shocked me. Remember when I had the flu and it lasted three weeks?'

Wheelan nodded. So Morgan did have more up his sleeve. It was a good job fate had taken a hand with the car crash that finished him off.

Mary went on, her demeanour softening. 'Well, I was recovering from the shock of it all and trying to work out what to do. Terry persuaded me that it was pointless to go to the police. I guess he was blackmailing me too at the time'.

Wheelan looked at Mary. He could see sadness and regret in her eyes for a brief moment.

'But that was a long time ago', she continued, her face lifting into an expression of determination once again.

They reached the manse and Mary returned the key to her handbag. She put the torch back in its place on the windowsill and continued peeling potatoes like nothing had happened. She was lost in her thoughts. Wheelan realised more than ever how good Mary was at keeping secrets and hiding her feelings. It was no wonder he'd failed to see through the secret Morgan had shared with her.

Wheelan wandered into the sitting room, gazing through the window at the beach. The tide was out and there were a few dog walkers enjoying the autumn sunshine they'd had recently. He saw Katie Halliday with that menace of a dog again and hoped she wouldn't call in. He couldn't face that – not today. Kids were not really his thing – not after his Kate had died in that tragic accident. His mind flashed with the thoughts of Kate as she must have been caught in the cave by the high spring tide. She had drowned alone and frightened. He pushed the thoughts away. He'd grieved for his daughter long enough.

Wheelan felt angry. All these years Morgan had terrorised him and that had been bad enough, but to know that Mary had been in on it too was hard to take. Admittedly she'd only known about Morgan's murder victims just before he died – or so she says – but why hadn't she told him? She was forever gossiping about everyone else. How the hell did she manage to keep that to herself?

And her knowing about the drug dealing – that must have been going on for a long time. If Morgan was paying her to keep quiet, that would have been an incentive, he supposed, but it was just so callous of her to keep up the pretence for so long.

He'd always thought of Mary as a friend. He believed she genuinely cared about him. But this just proved that she valued money over her loyalty to him. Wheelan wondered how much Morgan had paid her – how much it was worth to her to betray him like this. He felt deceived and angry.

'Lucas?' Mary was calling from the kitchen.

Sod off, Wheelan thought. He didn't answer.

She called again.

Determined silence…

Wheelan heard her stepping up behind him as he stared unseeingly through the sitting room window. He was simmering with resentment at Mary's duplicity. He spun round, his eyes now dark and menacing. 'Leave me alone Mary. Just get out and leave me alone'.

Mary started to protest but she saw the look in his eyes and simply nodded and turned to leave. She knew he'd had enough for one day.

Soon she was driving off up the slipway and out of sight.

Wheelan sighed deeply. He felt let down. His only friend had betrayed him. He'd cared about her in his own way but she'd wanted far more from their relationship than he was willing to give. Now everything was ruined…

Wheelan glanced at the clock. It was early afternoon but already he was craving his whiskey. He wandered out to the kitchen to distract himself and saw that Mary had left the peeled potatoes in a pan of cold water on the stove. There was also a beef casserole ready for the oven.

Could he trust her? He decided that if she was capable of deceiving him for so long, she was capable of poisoning him too. Now he'd sussed out her depraved plan, she'd turned to blackmail instead.

In a fit of temper, Wheelan grabbed the pan, tipped out the water and tossed the potatoes in the bin. Then he scraped the casserole in on top of them. There was no way he'd eat anything she prepared ever again. He'd get a take-away later. Bloody woman! He snarled.

The penetrating ring of the phone in the hall made him jump. He went to answer it. 'Yes?' he said abruptly.

'It's me', he instantly recognised Mary's voice.

'Leave me alone', was all Wheelan could say. He was still angry with her.

'I just wanted to see if you were alright. We need to talk properly'.

'Fuck off', Wheelan spat down the phone and cut her off before she could say more.

Wheelan was wound up like a spring. He was livid with Mary and utterly disappointed with himself. Why hadn't he seen this coming? Mary had been getting far too familiar with him for months – she'd obviously decided it was time to pounce. At least he'd found out about the poison. There was no way she could kill him off now, and he wouldn't marry her if she was the last woman on Earth.

Wheelan went back into the sitting room clutching his abdomen. His stomach hurt and he felt nauseous again. Damn the bitch and damn Morgan to hell – if he wasn't there already.

Sod it, Wheelan thought, he needed a drink, whatever hour of the day it was.

He pulled out a new bottle of whiskey from his stash in the sitting room cabinet. He wouldn't trust an opened bottle again. Mary could easily have tampered with it. He snapped the seal and poured himself a large measure in his favourite crystal glass. He took a large quaff of the fiery liquid and began to calm down. The booze would help him forget what an absolute mess his life had turned out to be.

Perhaps it would kill the pain too.

He took another mouthful, settling into his ancient armchair by the window, gazing out to sea.

Thirty minutes later and the pain in his stomach was much worse. The whiskey wasn't helping and the nausea was overwhelming.

Irritated, he put the glass down on the coffee table and ran up the stairs.

He made it to the bathroom just in time to vomit into the toilet. He noticed fresh blood and that same metallic taste he'd had after he puked up the cake in the graveyard the other day. He wiped his mouth and flushed, then reached for a bottle of antacid in the bathroom cabinet. He took a big swig from the bottle. Within a few minutes, the pain had eased slightly but he felt weak and listless.

Wheelan decided to have a lie down on the bed. He was exhausted with everything that had transpired over the past few days. The revelations from Mary, the drug addict he'd murdered and now this stomach pain intensifying. Was this what arsenic did to you, he thought? Hopefully he would start to feel better now he'd caught Mary out.

He kicked off his shoes and lay down, his pillow soft and welcoming.

He slipped gratefully into a deep, dreamless sleep…

+++

It was eleven o'clock in the evening when Wheelan woke to feel someone's body lying close behind him, a chubby arm tight around his chest. He could feel warm breath on his neck and a familiar flowery perfume.

'Bloody hell, Mary – what are you doing!' He pushed her arm away and sat bolt upright, turning to see Mary looking up at him from his bed.

'I just wanted to see that you were OK. You were angry with me earlier'.

'Yes and I'm still angry with you. Why can't you just leave me alone?' Wheelan felt exasperated with her. She just wouldn't get the message.

'Lucas I love you and I want us to be together – you know like a proper couple'. Mary's voice was wining and irritating.

'I've told you that it's not going to happen'. Wheelan slid to the edge of the bed, trying to distance himself from her.

Mary was silent for a moment before she spoke. 'My darling, I don't want to turn you into the police – not really. I just want you to see that we're meant to be together'. Her voice was infuriatingly jovial.

Wheelan glanced at her over his shoulder. 'Well you've got a funny way of showing it! You're bloody deranged, woman'.

He went on. 'What did you think you were going to achieve? Did you honestly think I would let you live here and allow you to slobber all over me just because you knew about what went on in the past? Things that had nothing to do with you?'

Mary started to look dejected but his anger was resurfacing. Dear God, the situation was getting way out of hand. He'd have to put a stop to it somehow.

Wheelan stood up and walked toward the stairs. He was going to finish off that whiskey first. He needed it, even if it did cause him pain.

Mary followed him.

As they reached the top of the stairs, she grabbed his arm. 'Please Lucas, think about it. We could be happy. We can put all this behind us'.

Wheelan's patience suddenly snapped. He spun round and gripped her firmly by both shoulders, shaking her furiously. Her chubby cheeks were wobbling and her eyes were staring wildly at him in surprise.

'For God's sake, woman; leave me alone'. He was shouting now and clearly enraged.

He felt his anger build to breaking point...

His heightened emotions left him dazed and disorientated but before he could think straight, he pushed her forcefully away from him before letting go.

She stumbled, unable to gain her footing.

As if in slow motion, Mary tried to grab the bannister as she toppled over the top stair.

She missed.

Her head hit the sixth stair down with a sickening thud and she fell headlong, crashing into each wooden step as she pounded down the staircase of the manse.

Her shrill scream was almost deafening...

Mary's body twisted awkwardly as it bounced off the staircase. Her head crashed sickeningly against the floor as she finally came to a stop at the bottom of the stairs.

Her head was resting on the hall tiles; her lower body still inclined up the bottom few stairs.

Her neck was twisted awkwardly and a small pool of blood seeped from beneath the crack in her skull...

Her left leg was bent out into an unnatural position.

She was shocked, distressed and calling for help.

Wheelan froze as he watched Mary tumble headlong down the stairs. Did he push her or was it an accident? He was in such a blind rage he couldn't recall the exact details.

He stood for long seconds, unable to move. He could hear her wails and her pleading with him for help.

Finally, he walked slowly and deliberately down each stair, trying to take stock of the situation. He held tightly on the balustrade to steady himself. Wheelan could see Mary was in agony and it looked like she had broken her leg. He saw the blood pooling on the tiles.

It matched the colour of her lipstick, he thought.

Mary's face was contorted into a vision of pain and disbelief. She was mouthing words but Wheelan could barely take it in.

What should he do?

'Call an ambulance, Lucas, quickly', Mary was saying between wails of agony.

Wheelan stood over her at the bottom of the stairs.

Her voice was growing weaker as she pleaded with him. Her staring eyes were beseeching him to help her.

He could call an ambulance.

Or let her die…

Chapter eight: ghosts of the past

Jenny had tried to talk to Mike after the incident with Bob at the hospital but he'd been even more remote and short-tempered with her. He'd dashed off after he'd hit Bob and had been very late getting home that evening with no explanations as to where he had been. She hadn't asked. It would only set off another argument. They'd gone to bed without talking things through and this morning, he'd barely spoken to her or Katie.

Something was wrong, Jenny thought. She'd never know him to behave like this. Normally he was calm, happy and reasonable and a genuinely nice person to have around but the last few days, he'd been moody and withdrawn, snapping at everything she said and now this outburst with Bob. She had to admit it had begun when he'd found out about his father's terminal cancer. Perhaps it was just a reaction to the devastating news. Jenny knew something like this could affect people in different ways. Perhaps withdrawing into himself was Mike's way of coping.

Mike was standing near the kitchen doorway, finishing off his breakfast of raspberry jam on toast before getting off to work. He was looking tired and drawn. Perhaps the extra responsibilities at work were getting the better of him, Jenny thought. She'd be glad when Mr Westland was back and Mike could step down. He needed a break to come to terms with his father's condition.

Jenny went to him and leaned in to kiss him but he pulled away. She felt hurt. Had things really become so bad that he was unwilling to give his wife a kiss goodbye? They needed one another at a time like this and Jenny was upset too at the news of her father-in-law's illness. What about her needs, she thought.

Mike took a final sip of his coffee and grabbed his briefcase. 'Sorry, Jenny, I have to go – I'm late'. He gave her an apologetic glance and left the cottage, calling up the stairs to Katie before pulling the front door shut.

Jenny heard his car roar into life and then he was gone.

Tears pricked her eyes. She felt sad and lonely. Why was Mike behaving like this? Why was he pushing her away at the very time they needed each other? Was it the thing with Bob? They had discussed it when Bob first started pestering her a few months ago. Mike knew she wasn't the slightest bit interested in her ex-husband – she found his behaviour frustrating and very unwelcome and she'd tried her best to get him to leave her alone. But Bob was persistent. He was sending her jokey text messages and leaving voicemails on her phone but it was all harmless enough – certainly nothing that should cause Mike to react so strongly.

Jenny felt a wrenching pang of guilt that Bob's nose had been broken and that she'd walked off without even checking he was OK. She'd heard nothing more from him and assumed he'd got it looked at in Accident and Emergency. Perhaps he'd finally gotten the message to leave her alone. The two men reminded her of a couple of silly schoolboys in a playground fight. But what on Earth could she do about it?

Jenny made a second cup of tea and ambled into the conservatory. She was working on the surgical ward again later that day but had a few hours before her shift started. She decided to have a quiet morning with Katie and the dogs so she relaxed into the sofa and took in the panoramic view before her. The sea was mirror calm and shafts of golden sunlight danced across the surface of the water. The tide was full in and gentle waves lapped the beach. Oystercatchers were running up and down with the movements of the water as they foraged for food on the shoreline. It was a picture of serenity and peace. But Jenny felt anything but serene. Her emotions were in turmoil with all that was going on. Why was Mike shutting her out? Was it something she'd inadvertently said to upset him? Was it simply a reaction to his father's sudden announcement?

Or was there something else going on…

Jenny began to think about the way Mike had been acting over the past few months – well before his father's devastating news or Bob's foolish antics. He'd been late home several times without a plausible explanation. Sure, he'd taken on extra responsibilities at work but that didn't really explain everything. It didn't explain the times he hadn't come home until almost midnight or the expensive new suit and shirts he'd bought recently – normally he was happy in his old jeans and t-shirts. He wasn't a suit man at all. Maybe he wasn't the person she thought he was after all.

Jenny felt almost guilty that she was beginning to mistrust him but could it be that Mike was having an affair? It wasn't like him to deceive her and he didn't seem the type to have an affair – if there was a type. She hadn't believed Bob could betray her either, yet he had and it had ended their marriage.

Jenny hated herself for even considering that her wonderful husband could hurt her like that. Surely Mike wouldn't risk losing all they'd built together over the years. Jenny reasoned it must be the stress of his father's illness that was making him moody and withdrawn. He must have called in to see his father last evening. That must have been why he was late home, she reasoned.

Jenny thought of John Halliday and realised she'd meant to call him yesterday but had forgotten with the drama of Mike's fracas with Bob. She would call him, she thought, and John would tell her that Mike had been there. That would settle her mind and she could stop all the wild speculation.

She reached for the phone. John answered after three rings.

'Hi, Dad, how are you? I just thought I'd check you were alright before I go to work this afternoon'.

'Oh, not too bad, love. I'm sure I'll be fine now'. His voice trailed off as if he'd said something he shouldn't have.

'Oh good – has something happened? Have you had another opinion?' Jenny asked, anticipating some good news.

John hesitated before answering. 'Err no love. I just meant I'll be ok. Don't worry about me'. John sounded strange, as if he was hiding something.

Jenny started to probe further but John deftly cut her off, quickly changing the subject.

'Are you working with Mike today?' He asked.

Jenny didn't want to ask awkward questions and let it lie. 'Yes I'm on Mike's ward later. It's the only time I get to see him lately', she said jovially. 'You know what it's like working shifts'.

'Yes, I remember those days. Say hello to him for me and Martha – we haven't seen him much either but I know he's been busy lately. Perhaps we'll see you both on the weekend'. John said.

Jenny realised that Mike hadn't been to his father's after all. So where the hell had he been until nearly midnight?

Jenny chatted with John a little longer and they hung up, promising to get in touch again soon.

Far from settling her mind, the conversation with her father-in-law had made her feel even more anxious. There was still the question of where Mike had been last evening – and all the other evenings he'd been late – but there was something else. John had sounded decidedly cagey, as if he was hiding something from her. She knew him well enough to sense when something was awry. Perhaps Mike had confided in him and told him something that she wasn't supposed to know.

What if he'd told his father he was having an affair?

Jenny felt sick with apprehension. She had no evidence whatsoever to confront Mike with but there was definitely something wrong. She would have to keep a careful eye on how things developed. If necessary, she'd have to ask Mike outright where he'd been and what he'd been up to all those evenings he'd been late home. She didn't intend to be confrontational but she couldn't bear to go through all the heartache and turmoil of a husband's unfaithfulness again. She had to know. It had been bad enough when Bob had cheated on her with her so called friend, Isobel, but this was too much. She loved Mike to distraction and now they had a child to consider as well. Jenny felt deflated and angry at the thought of being betrayed a second time by someone she loved.

The shrill ring of the phone cut into her thoughts. Perhaps it was John calling back to reassure her?

'Hello is that Jenny Barratt?' a woman's voice said.

'Yes'.

'It's Sandra from the nursing agency. I was wondering if you could do us a favour. We have you down for a shift this afternoon at the hospital but I was wondering if you'd be able to call in on an old lady on your way. She lives near you and her regular nurse has gone off sick. It's just to make sure she's ok and change her dressing. Could you manage it?'

'Sure, no problem', Jenny said.

Jenny made a note of the lady's details. Her name was Gillian Baxter and she was eighty-nine years old. She lived alone on the outskirts of the village, tucked away down a private lane. Jenny had never been to that area but she knew where it was. It wouldn't take long to get there.

Katie came downstairs at the sound of Jenny's voice on the phone again, Barney at her side. 'Mum can I read to you before you go to work? I have to practice for school'.

'Of course you can sweetheart. Bring your book and we'll sit here'. Jenny said; glad to spend time with her daughter.

Katie fetched her reading book and snuggled up next to her mother. Jenny put her arm around her little girl and they smiled at one another, content to be together. Katie began reading a fanciful story about witches and hobgoblins with perfect inflection in her voice and flawless reading of the more difficult words. She was a clever child; advanced for her years. Barney settled himself on the floor at their feet. Treacle lay stretched out in front of the picture window and they could hear Honey snoring loudly from her basket in the kitchen.

Jenny forgot her troubles as she immersed herself in Katie's reading.

All too soon, Laura arrived and it was time for Jenny to leave for work via Mrs Baxter's house. As ever, she felt the familiar reluctance to leave Katie but she forced herself to get ready and leave the cottage.

Katie and Barney saw her to the front door and Jenny kissed Katie's soft cheek. 'I love you sweetheart. See you later', she said. Jenny smoothed Barney's silky coat. 'See you soon too Barney'.

Jenny waved to her little family as she drove off up the lane from the cottage. Thankfully, her apprehension about Mike's uncharacteristic behaviour had faded into the background as she focused on the task at hand. She turned right at the main coast road and headed inland. Soon, she reached the private driveway that led from the main road to Gillian Baxter's house. The narrow driveway snaked deeper into the countryside, lined on either side by tall hedges. After two hundred yards, the driveway opened out into a courtyard. To the left stood a detached double fronted Georgian style house with a porch and a blue front door. A stone wall with a central gate marked the boundary of the front garden.

Jenny froze.

She knew this house!

Yet she had never been here before or even been able to see down the long driveway to glimpse the building – it was completely obscured from the road by tall trees and hedges. Jenny looked up to see the attic window to the right of the roof and then she remembered. It was the image of Katie's painting. Even the detail of the colours and the bushy tree to the right of the house were perfectly accurate.

This was creepy, Jenny thought. How could Katie have known what this house looked like? Perhaps she'd walked down the lane with her father on one of their weekend jaunts with the dogs. Katie certainly wouldn't have come here alone – she was too young to be walking along the main road and she always stuck to the slipway to the beach.

Jenny slowly got out of her car, the spine-chilling feeling refusing to go away. She opened the gate and walked up the short cobbled pathway that led to the front door. She rang the bell and waited. Through the frosted glass of the door, she saw the silhouette of an old woman shuffling her way down the hallway. She unbolted the heavy wooden door and it creaked open.

Gillian Baxter stood slightly bent over in the doorway. 'You must be nurse Barrett', she said sternly. 'The agency said you were coming – I hope you're going to do a good job of my dressing. The last nurse they sent made a right hash of it'. The woman's face was set into a critical scowl that had probably developed over many years.

Jenny stood transfixed. She'd never seen this obnoxious woman in her life, yet she felt as if she already knew her.

It wasn't a pleasant experience...

'Well, don't just stand there, come in. You're already late'. Her tone was unnecessarily brusque.

Jenny felt a sense of foreboding as she was ushered into the house. Actually, she wasn't late and she didn't like the way she'd been greeted. The old lady clearly wasn't a very nice person, Jenny thought.

She was led into a large living room. It was cold and smelt damp and musty. The furniture was as ancient as the old lady and there were piles of clutter everywhere. The old woman slumped into her armchair with an exaggerated sigh, making it obvious Jenny was an utter nuisance for making her get up to answer the door.

Jenny felt deeply uncomfortable in this room. It seemed spookily familiar but the atmosphere was definitely hostile. She tried to block the feeling and focus on her patient. She was here to do a job. 'What can I do for you Mrs Baxter?' Jenny asked, trying hard to remain pleasant.

'You'll have to change my dressing', she said, lifting her skirt to reveal a bandaged lower right leg. 'It's my varicose ulcers and they just don't seem to be healing'. She plonked her foot on a low footstool in front of her.

'OK, I'll have a look at that for you. Where are your new dressings and your notes?' Jenny asked.

The old woman pointed to a long rosewood dresser running the length of the wall in front of her. It was filled with trinkets, a myriad of old photos and piles of papers – all covered in a thick layer of dust. At one end of the dresser was a box of dressings. Jenny went over to get them and stopped dead in her tracks as one of the pictures caught her eye. She leaned in to get a better look. It was a faded black and white photograph of two young teenagers, a dour looking sandy-haired boy and a smiling girl with long dark hair. It was obviously a very old photograph. Jenny had the eerie feeling that she knew the girl. Her face was so familiar, yet she couldn't place her. She also sensed she'd seen the boy before too. Still puzzled, she grabbed the box of dressings and the nursing notes and went back to her patient.

Jenny quickly reviewed the notes and snapped on a pair of latex gloves from the box. She spread some newspaper beneath Mrs Baxter's leg and knelt before her to unwrap the old bandages. 'Right, let's get this old dressing off shall we?' Jenny said brightly.

The woman nodded wearily in reply, scrutinising Jenny as she got to work.

The stench from the ulcers was putrid and Jenny tried hard not to gag as she unwound layer upon layer of bandage to reveal a dressing pad soaked with vile pus and fluid. She carefully peeled off the pad and wrapped it with the bandage in the newspaper ready to be incinerated.

'This must be painful for you', Jenny said looking up at the old woman. She could swear she knew her from somewhere too.

Mrs Baxter was still scowling. 'Yes it is painful but the dressings help'. She said, a little more kindly.

Jenny prepared a dressing pack ready to clean the wounds and changed her gloves for fresh sterile ones. There were three nasty looking ulcers that had eaten into her patient's flesh and there was a lot of thick pus and dead tissue that needed to be debrided from the wound. Jenny got to work cleaning the ulcers with a forceps and cotton wool soaked in a sterile saline solution. Her patient winced with pain once or twice but didn't complain. She appeared to be well used to the procedure. The leg was swollen and oedematous and the skin looked red and sore from varicose eczema associated with this type of leg ulcer. She dabbed the skin dry with a sterile paper towel from the pack.

'I'll rub some emollient into this', Jenny said, reaching for a large pot of aqueous cream.

'That's soothing', the old woman said as Jenny applied the cream. She seemed more pleasant now, her distrust of Jenny starting to fade. 'You were looking at that photograph', she said nodding toward the cabinet.

'Yes, the young couple just reminded me of someone, but I can't think who', Jenny said as she gently massaged the cream into Mrs Baxter's leg.

'That's my niece and her boyfriend. He didn't last long – a bit of a thug, even as a kid. I don't know what she saw in him. But that was many years ago. He since died in a car accident and good riddance to him – he turned out to be a bad 'un'. The old woman scowled again.

'What's your niece's name? She's a pretty girl', Jenny asked.

'Helen'. She said bluntly.

Jenny felt decidedly uneasy but couldn't understand why. 'Does Helen live nearby? Does she come to visit you?' The girl in the photo was intriguing her; perhaps she'd passed her in the village.

Mrs Baxter waved her arm as if to dismiss her niece. 'She disappeared one dark night and I never saw her again. Don't know what happened to her'.

'Oh dear, that's a shame. Were you close?' Jenny asked as she reached for a dressing pad.

'No not really', Mrs Baxter said. 'She lived with us for a while after her parents died in a car crash but she used to shut herself away in her room in the attic for hours on end. My husband didn't like her at all and they were forever quarrelling. I think she just ran away'. The woman's voice trailed off.

Jenny's blood ran cold as she applied the dressing pad to the leg ulcers. Helen must be the face in the attic window of Katie's painting. This was all too weird, Jenny thought.

She tried to concentrate on dressing her patient's leg, fighting a feeling of mounting apprehension. Jenny applied a light gauze bandage to keep the dressing in place then began winding a compression bandage around Mrs Baxter's leg.

'Not too tight', the woman said sternly.

Jenny loosened the tension slightly on the bandage and continued.

Mrs Baxter was scowling once more. 'My husband was a cruel man. I saw him hit her several times. It's no wonder she went off like that. To tell you the truth, I think she was pregnant and afraid she'd get a beating if he found out'. The woman leaned forward to inspect the bandaging. 'Yes that's more comfortable now', she said.

Jenny came to the end of the bandage and fastened it securely. Her hands were trembling as she fought to control the strange feeling of trepidation that was overpowering her. The more the old woman spoke about Helen, the more anxious she felt. It was as if she could feel what Helen must have felt at the hands of her uncle.

She tried to snap out of it.

Jenny had experienced a heightened sense of intuition since her near death experience but nothing as forceful as this. She felt an unfamiliar and intense empathy with Helen.

She felt certain she knew this place – this house – and she knew this belligerent woman...

Then as if she was being transposed to another world, Jenny felt Helen's pain and loneliness acutely as she pictured her shutting herself away in the attic. It was as if she *was* Helen.

Did she hide herself away or was she locked in from the outside? Jenny sensed that Helen had been kept an unwilling prisoner in that barren attic room.

In her ghostly vision, she experienced Helen's fear with frightening realism as her uncle beat her remorselessly; over and over again. She felt the sting of his belt as it slashed against her legs and the unbearable pain as the metal buckle bit into her flesh.

Jenny felt Helen's terrifying urgency to get away as if it were actually happening to her now.

Helen *was* pregnant – Jenny could sense it – and she knew she'd escaped and fled from this very house to save her unborn baby from the depravity of her aunt and uncle.

'Are you alright, nurse?' Mrs Baxter was asking. 'You look as if you've seen a ghost'.

Jenny felt as if she had indeed seen a ghost.

The ghost of Helen...

Jenny realised Helen was dead. How did she die? What had happened to her and her baby?

She couldn't sense how Helen's life had ended but she had experienced the conscious awareness of Helen's spirit as if it were her own for a few fleeting moments.

Was Helen reaching out to her from beyond the grave? Was she trying to tell her what had happened?

Jenny knew that life continued after death and she'd experienced for herself the ability to see from a vantage point outside her body.

Could Helen see her now in her aunt's house?

Was she somehow projecting her thoughts and feelings onto Jenny?

Jenny had to get out of there. She had to get away from Helen's aunt and from this detestable house.

She saw this loathsome woman before her and had felt herself being transported to the past.

Her past...

Jenny wasn't sensing Helen's presence.

She *was* Helen...

Chapter nine: broken mind

Wheelan sat on the bottom stair next to Mary. She was still writhing in agony. It had been over three hours now and Wheelan had still not called an ambulance. He wasn't sure he wanted to.

Mary had been pleading with him desperately to help her but now she was calmer and seemed resigned to her uncertain fate. Her hip was fractured but the pool of blood around her head was congealing. She was obviously weak but still conscious.

Wheelan was ready to talk. He had to sort this mess out. He was the one in control now and he'd make sure she listened to him. There were questions to be asked and he needed answers so he could finally sort out the chaos that was going on in his mind.

'How could you have poisoned me Mary?' Wheelan still couldn't grasp why someone that supposedly loved him would deliberately make him ill.

Mary turned her head slowly and looked at Wheelan, her eyes dejected. 'I haven't been poisoning you – honestly. I keep telling you'. Her voice was barely a whisper.

'You say you care about me and yet you put arsenic in my food. Was it to make me ill so I would become dependent on you? It's a medical condition, Mary. You can get help for it'.

Mary reached out to touch Wheelan's arm. 'No – I promise, I haven't been giving you anything'. Mary sounded exasperated but her voice was feeble.

'It'll be in your bag', Wheelan said as he stood up and strode toward the kitchen, determined to find the evidence.

Mary's voluminous handbag was on the kitchen table and Wheelan snatched it, tipping out the contents. He sifted through her purse, her diary and make up. The iron key to the cavern spilled out and there were paper tissues and sticky sweets but no arsenic. He scanned through her diary but there was nothing but mundane appointments and shopping lists.

Wheelan wandered back to the hall, pacing back and forth. Mary was still lying helplessly at the foot of the stairs.

He glanced at the phone. Should he call an ambulance? Not yet. He still needed answers…

'So you knew about the drug dealing. What was the arrangement with Morgan?' Wheelan kept pacing steadily back and forth.

'Please Lucas, get help. I'm in agony'. Mary reached her arm out to him, beseeching.

'What was the deal?' He said bluntly.

Mary withdrew her arm in defeat. 'Terry paid me £1,000 a month to keep an eye on you'.

Wheelan stopped pacing and looked at Mary. '£1,000 a month? That's all it took for you to betray me?'

'I needed the money to keep a roof over our heads and put my boy through collage. It was tough after Colin died. He left us with no money, no insurance. Please get some help'. Mary was panting her words out, obviously exhausted and in pain.

'You could have come to me. I could have helped you. Why did you take money from that bastard?'

'I was embarrassed to ask for help at the time', Mary said weakly, 'I always thought we'd be together – I lived in hope of that. Taking money from Terry was always going to be a temporary arrangement. I didn't think it would go on for so long'.

'So it's my fault now is it?' Wheelan asked. He resumed his pacing of the hall.

'No, of course not. But we *did* need the money and I couldn't turn it down. It just became a habit'. Mary looked up at Wheelan. 'I'm sorry', she said.

'What else do you know?' Wheelan asked.

'Nothing – honestly. It was just about the money. Please help me. Call an ambulance'. Mary's voice was faltering.

'What about these boys that Morgan killed? You were quite happy to pin that on me'. Wheelan changed tack, sensing he was beginning to soften up with Mary's reasoning. She did seem to be genuinely telling the truth.

'Oh Lucas, I was desperate for you to want me. I'd have said anything. Do you really believe I'd have you put away? I was clutching at straws. If I wanted to see you in jail, I could have done it a long time ago'. Mary was struggling to find the breath to talk. 'Please get some help'.

'If you and Morgan were so chummy, what else was going on? Were you sleeping with him?' Morgan felt weirdly jealous.

'Don't be silly, Lucas, of course not. I was in love with you. I always have been'. Mary looked at him pleadingly.

He saw the truth in her eyes. It was a ridiculous idea, he thought. Morgan avoided complications; he'd only ever been interested in prostitutes.

Apart from Helen all those years ago…

He reeled when he remembered how Helen had been taken in by the young Morgan's charms – if only briefly – yet she hadn't realised *he* existed. Wheelan had been besotted with her and Morgan had taken her from him.

Mary cut into his thoughts. 'We were like a family, don't you remember – you and I and little Kate. We could have been a happy family. I wanted that so much, Lucas'. Mary closed her eyes, tears threatening to spill down her chubby cheeks. 'I loved you more than anything in the world, but you wouldn't love me back'. Her voice was weak and breaking with emotion.

Wouldn't or couldn't, Wheelan thought.

In his younger days, he could almost see them together, yet something always held him back. He cared about Mary but maybe just not in the way she wanted. His tortured soul was incapable of loving another person, yet he'd known Mary was waiting for him to declare his love. He'd deliberately withheld his deepest feelings and kept her living on the very edge of hope. It suited him that way. He'd denied her real happiness in order to serve his own selfish needs. She was almost a prisoner, waiting for a love he could never give. He should have released her to find someone else – someone who would love her as she deserved to be loved.

Wheelan now realised now how much Mary had cared about him. Yet he had constantly rejected her.

And what about him? The stable family life he'd once craved in his youth had been there for the taking but he was blind to it. What had he been so afraid of? He looked at Mary lying at the foot of the stairs, the blood around her head, her leg broken. She was sobbing. Her bosom was heaving with torrents of inconsolable grief for the life they could have had.

Wheelan couldn't watch her.

His earlier anger had dissipated and guilt had inadvertently crept up on him.

He could see it now…

He was the reason she'd been so unhappy. He'd kept her dangling on a string because it suited his egotistical needs. If he'd been there for her as a true friend, she wouldn't have had to turn to Morgan for financial help. If he'd welcomed her into his home, it would have eased the hardship and loneliness she'd felt after her husband's death.

It was true. They *had* felt like a family when they took in baby Kate – his baby – after she was abandoned in the chapel. He'd brutally murdered her mother, yet Mary had been a devoted surrogate. She'd loved Kate as much as she loved her own children, yet he held back, unable or unwilling to let her into his heart.

He knew now that Mary didn't know about Helen. She hadn't believed for a moment that he was a killer and she must never know…

Wheelan paced the hall and went into the sitting room. He needed a few minutes alone to sort out the jumbled feelings that were cascading through his mind. He gazed out of the window to see the darkness of night beginning to fade, the clouds in the eastern sky blushing pink at the start of a new day.

It was clear to him now. Mary genuinely did care about him. It was ridiculous to think she'd been blackmailing or poisoning him. She'd simply been desperate to get through to him. He should have listened…

He'd let her down but perhaps it wasn't too late to put things right. Maybe their friendship at least could survive these extraordinary revelations and even go on to become stronger now the truth was out in the open. For all his doubts, he couldn't really imagine his life without Mary in it. Not after all these years.

He knew what he had to do…

Wheelan went over and sat next to her again on the bottom stair. She had her eyes closed and her cheeks were wet and glistening with tears. He silently took her hand in his. He had some apologising to do.

But her hand was lifeless and limp.

Wheelan grabbed Mary by the shoulders once again and shook her gently.

There was no response.

'No Mary, wait – don't die'.

Her mouth gaped open.

It was too late.

Mary was dead…

Chapter ten: betrayal

Jenny left Mrs Baxter's house as quickly as she could. The old woman must have thought her rude but Jenny had no intention of going back there – ever. She'd driven part way down the winding driveway until she was out of sight of the house and stopped the car. She was shaken after the vivid flashback of her previous lifetime as Helen. It had been chillingly intense.

Jenny tried to shake off the feeling. She just wished her life would get back to normal. Why had she been given this alarming ability to sense things from the past?

Jenny took a deep breath and forced herself to calm down. She had to reason with this logically. Had Katie experienced some sort of premonition when she painted the picture of Mrs Baxter's house? Katie had said something about it being the house that Jenny had lived in before Katie had been born. Yet how did she know? She'd painted the details of the house incredibly accurately. Jenny found it unnerving yet fascinating.

Jenny took a deep breath and tried to refocus on the here and now. She spent hours sometimes, contemplating unanswered questions; yet she had to concentrate now and get on with her day.

At times, she longed to re-visit the ethereal realm that had embraced and intrigued her – where she'd felt so much at home. She'd wanted to stay, yet she had been persuaded to return to live in the physical world. Sometimes Jenny found it difficult to stay grounded.

There had been so much happening lately with the bombshell of John's terminal cancer, Mike's uncharacteristic moodiness and the silly incident with Bob. Now with the vivid experience of reliving the emotional turmoil of a past life to deal with – she could barely think straight.

Jenny gripped the steering wheel tightly. She simply had to focus and get to the hospital or she'd be late for her shift. She took another deep breath, pushed the gear stick into first and started to drive off.

Her phone rang. She stopped again. It was Bob. He can sod off; she thought as she dismissed the call, she didn't have time or patience for him.

'Calm down and get to work', she repeated to herself as she pulled off once again.

As she drove along the coast toward the next town, the view of the sea and the salt air enveloped her senses. Gradually, she felt herself becoming grounded back into reality. Shafts of sunlight played on the water's surface and flocks of gulls squawked as they glided above the coast.

Jenny was much calmer as she reached the hospital and had forced herself to focus on the day ahead. She found a parking place and walked briskly toward the hospital entrance - she was only just in time for her shift.

As Jenny reached the hospital concourse, she spotted Mike in his theatre scrubs sitting at one of the coffee tables. He was with a woman who had her back to Jenny. She couldn't see who it was but they were deep in conversation. Compelled to know more, Jenny slowed down and dodged behind a large potted plant.

Her stomach lurched. What was he up to? Who was the woman he was with? Her suspicions about his recent behaviour were aroused once again as she watched him chatting with this rather elegant looking woman in a classy linen dress. So was this why he'd bought expensive new clothes, Jenny wondered?

A nursing colleague sidled up to Jenny. She'd noticed her spying on her husband. 'They've been getting *very* cosy lately! They were in here the other day too'. Her tone was gossipy and Jenny could see she was revelling in the assumptions she was making.

Jenny just glared at her as she walked off. Oh God, what if it was true, Jenny thought. What if he *was* having an affair with this woman? She chanced another peek through the leaves of the plant. They were still huddled over the coffee table, conspiring as if they were sharing a deep dark secret…

Just then a young man in a long black apron went over to their table with two drinks. He placed them on the table in front of them and as he was about to leave, the woman looked up at him. Jenny could clearly see her face from the side.

She gasped with shock.

It was Isobel.

The bitch, Jenny thought. The absolute bloody conniving bitch! She'd stolen Bob from her and now she was after her husband as well. How had she ever called her a friend?

Jenny was reeling from this new revelation. No wonder Mike had been distant and behaving so strangely lately. He must have been having an illicit affair with Isobel.

Jenny couldn't bring herself to witness any more. She was livid at Isobel and at Mike for their apparent betrayal. Why else would Isobel be having coffee with *her* husband? They were so brazen about it too – right in front of the whole hospital. She would be a laughing stock when this got out.

Perhaps Bob had been trying to warn her about it the other day. Mike could have punched him as a threat against saying anything. She had to speak to Bob and find out what was going on but she didn't want him to have the satisfaction of knowing her marriage was in trouble. She would pick her words carefully.

Jenny took another peek at Mike and Isobel from behind the plant. They were still in deep discussion about something. She darted out from behind the plant and quickly disappeared into the corridor. She felt angry and let down.

She checked her watch. She'd better hurry – she was now ten minutes late for her shift and she had to change into her scrubs yet. She wanted to stop and call Bob but there wasn't time. She'd have to sneak a call later when she had a chance.

Jenny changed and arrived at the ward office in a fluster. The nurses were having a staff handover and the ward sister glared at her accusingly from behind the desk.

'So sorry I'm late', Jenny said, scrambling to tie her hair back into a ponytail 'traffic was bad'. She could hardly tell them the truth, she thought.

Sister nodded in acknowledgement and continued with the staff handover. Jenny found a seat and listened intently as a summary of each patient's condition was given along with their treatment regime. She made a few hasty notes as a reminder.

Sister continued, 'Mr Evans' palpitations became so severe that we've transferred him to cardiothoracics.

He's being monitored as a precaution'. Sister said. 'In that bed instead, we now have Mrs Lipton. She's on this afternoon's list for a cholecystectomy. She'll need prepping for theatre – I'm afraid we've been too busy to do it this morning'.

Jenny was stunned at the development with Mr Evans. She wondered if his palpitations were due to the bravafloxacin. She would have to do some digging around to find out.

'Finally, we have Mr Blake, a fifty year old, three day post-op patient. He's had a liver carcinoma removed and is making satisfactory progress. He's to have a blood transfusion this afternoon for a low haemoglobin count. We have two units cross matched. Mr Halliday has also written him up for antibiotics for a slight chest infection – although personally, I don't think it's necessary. But who are we nurses to argue!'

Sister's remarks about Mike's prescribing seemed sarcastic and Jenny wondered if, in part, they were directed at her in retaliation for being late. She had to agree though. He had been overprescribing this new drug and she was yet to tackle him about it. That and the fact he'd been seen with Isobel. Things were not looking good, Jenny thought.

The nurses were allocated to their patients and they disbanded to make a start on the mountain of work that awaited them. Jenny began, as usual with her drug round and grabbed the keys to the medicine trolley. A junior nurse assisted her.

As she checked each patient's drug chart, she could see that Mike had prescribed 100mg of bravafloxacin to practically every patient on the ward, apart from one frail looking woman who was allergic to a long list of drugs and other substances.

She asked the patients how they were feeling and several admitted they felt nauseous and a few had itchy skin or light-headedness. One man, Mr Ridley, was visibly shaking and complaining of palpitations. Once again, his symptoms coincided with the start of the antibiotics. Jenny noticed that most of the patients that were complaining of symptoms were post-operative patients on analgesics such as ibuprofen, although some were taking diclofenac. It could indicate an adverse drug interaction.

It was all too much of a coincidence…

What the hell was going on, Jenny thought, and why had none of the other nurses or doctors questioned this? Sister didn't agree with the prescribing but she'd done nothing to address the issue. Jenny would have to speak to Mike about it herself.

An hour later, Mike appeared on the ward. Jenny saw him and a rush of resentment threatened to spill out into harsh words. She had to bite her tongue. This was neither the time nor place to have a stand up argument with her husband in front of a ward full of patients and staff. She'd have to wait until they were at home later before she confronted him about his behaviour and about Isobel. She could barely contain her anger, hurt and disappointment.

Jenny casually walked over to where Mike was sitting at the nurses' station. He was scrutinising an x-ray on the ward's computer. 'Hi Mike', she said as steadily as she could muster, although she could feel her voice faltering.

Mike looked up and smiled half-heartedly. 'Hi Jenny, how are things?'

'Not too bad', she lied, 'I need to speak to you about some of the patients'. She paused, waiting to get his full attention.

Mike turned in his chair to face her. 'What's the problem?' he asked.

'Practically everyone has been prescribed bravafloxacin but many patients are complaining of symptoms that seem to me like side effects – nausea, itchy skin and dizziness mainly. A few are having worrying palpitations and Mr Evans has had to go to cardiothoracics to be monitored because his arrhythmias were so severe. I'm wondering if it could be a drug reaction with the analgesia. Would you have a look at this please?' Jenny could see Mike was finally listening to her.

The surgeon considered what she'd said for a moment and nodded. 'OK, I'll have a look at them in a bit. I have to sort this out first'. He said, gesturing to the x-ray.

'Alright, thanks', Jenny said, relieved to have said her bit.

'It could be anything you know – not necessarily the antibiotics'. Mike was making light of her concerns.

At least she had told him and hopefully he would reconsider his recent prescribing strategy. Jenny wandered off to check on a post-op patient.

When she had finished recording her patient's blood pressure, she realised she had a few minutes to call Bob. She was eager to know what was going on with Isobel and maybe Bob could shed some light on the situation. Did he realise his girlfriend was having an affair? Jenny briefly thought it would be rough justice and maybe he deserved it if it were true. She sneaked

off the ward for a few minutes on the pretence she was going to fetch some results from the bacteriology lab.
When she reached the corridor, she dialled Bob's number.

'Hi, Jenny', Bob said. His voice sounded muffled.

'Hi Bob. Listen, sorry about the other day. Are you alright?'

'I've got a broken nose thanks to your arrogant husband but otherwise fine. What was all that about?' Bob asked. There didn't seem to be any resentment toward *her* in his tone.

'You tell me – I haven't a clue what came over him. I am sorry though. You didn't deserve that'. Jenny wasn't sure how to broach the Isobel thing but she decided to simply come out with it. 'So how are things with Isobel?' She waited, listening intently for Bob to answer.

Bob sighed. 'She left me a few months ago. It's finally over, Jenny'.

Jenny thought better than to react. It was a possible explanation for the way he'd been hounding her lately though.

'So where is she now?' Jenny said calmly, knowing full well where she was – with her husband!

'Oh, she decided she'd had enough of nursing and became a drug rep. She's travelling all over the West Country at the moment visiting doctors' surgeries and hospitals peddling her drugs. Making a good salary as well, so I hear'. Bob sounded peeved.

So; Jenny thought, Isobel had a job as a pharmaceutical rep. It didn't take a genius to put two and two together –

Mike was overprescribing to please her. She was shocked to think that Mike would jeopardise his career to keep his tarty little mistress happy. He must be helping her to reach her sales targets – at the expense of his patient's health.

This was way too much.

Jenny pried for more information but didn't succeed in getting any further with it. She chatted a little longer to Bob, apologising once more for his broken nose before hanging up.

Slowly she walked back to the surgical ward, contemplating the latest twist in her life. Today had turned out to be an emotional rollercoaster; what with the experience at Mrs Baxter's and now this. Jenny knew she had no choice but to confront Mike about Isobel. She would speak to him at home later.

As she reached the ward, she heard the pandemonium. One of the patients had crashed and gone into cardiac arrest. Nurses and doctors were rushing to the scene and Jenny too hurried over to the patient's bed. It was Mr Ridley, the patient that had complained of palpitations earlier. Mike had got to him swiftly and was performing cardiac compressions.

One of the resuscitation team, an anaesthetist, had tilted the patient's head back, applied a bag-mask to his nose and mouth and was bagging him with artificial respirations.

A nurse was hurriedly attaching electrocardiogram leads to the heart monitor and a junior doctor was firing up a manual defibrillator, the wining of the machine indicating it was charging.

'Draw up the adrenaline, Jenny, and stand by with the atropine', Mike called breathlessly to her.

Jenny went over to the arrest trolley and found a glass ampule of adrenaline. She broke the ampule and drew up a standard 1mg dose of adrenaline into a syringe. She removed the needle and handed the syringe to one of the doctors standing at the bedside. They checked the dosage on the ampule and the doctor gave the life-saving drug to the patient intravenously.

A nurse placed two pads of conducting gel, one on the upper right chest and the other above the left ribcage, ready for defibrillation.

'Clear', the junior doctor said as he slammed the defibrillator paddles onto the man's chest.

Mike and the anaesthetist stepped back and the electrical charge was delivered. The patient convulsed as the shock surged through his chest and into his failing heart.

Mike checked the ECG on the monitor screen. 'He's still in VF', he said.

He started cardiac compressions again as the junior doctor ramped up the charge on the defibrillator. The machine started its wining noise once more.

'Clear', the junior doctor called again.

Everyone stepped back as he slammed the paddles onto Mr Ridley's chest for the second time.

The patient convulsed with the shock. This time his heart monitor showed the trace of his restored heartbeat, a rhythmic beeping coming from the machine.

'He's back', Mike called. 'We've got sinus rhythm'. He looked over at Jenny, relief written all over his face. He handed the patient over to the anaesthetist – he would need careful monitoring in case of a relapse.

Mike strode over to the nurses' station, his fingers raking through his dark blonde hair. He looked troubled.

Jenny rushed after him. 'Mike', she said in a hushed tone, 'he was complaining of palpitations earlier. I'm convinced it's the bravafloxacin'.

She waited for him to reply...

Jenny searched deeply into her husband's olive green eyes as he turned to her.

'I think you might be right'.

Chapter eleven: regrets

Wheelan paced for more than an hour, contemplating what to do. Mary was dead and it was all his fault. She still lay twisted and broken at the foot of the stairs, a pool of blood drying on the hall tiles. Her red lipstick was clown-like against the deathly pallor of her skin.

He could have called an ambulance immediately and saved her life, but he'd been too wrapped up in his own wretched emotional state to do what was right for Mary.

He'd let her die and now he hated himself for what he had done.

Wheelan glanced out of the sitting room window. It had been a long night but dawn was approaching fast. He'd have to act soon. He could see Mary's car still parked on the gravel driveway outside the manse.

He could still call an ambulance. It wasn't too late. He could say he'd been sleeping and hadn't heard her fall down the stairs. Wheelan wondered if that was plausible. How could anyone sleep through something like that? Maybe he was drunk or had taken something to help him sleep. That would do it. He could say he'd woken in the morning to find her dead at the bottom of the stairs. There would be gossip around the village but he could cope with that. It was no secret that Mary spent a lot of time at the manse – she *had* worked for him as a housekeeper for many years. Wheelan knew his life was about to change drastically.

Should he call an ambulance?

Wheelan paced the sitting room and out into the kitchen. He was still in shock. An ambulance couldn't help her now and what if the police came sniffing around? That was inevitable, surely, he thought. They would come to question him. What if they found something to implicate him in Mary's death? What if they searched the place? There were too many secrets to uncover – the youth he'd murdered, Morgan's dead victims. What if they did pin the boys' murders on him? Then there was the stash of heroin and cocaine that he was still dealing. All it would take would be for some dead-beat drug addict to snitch on him and that would be it. His life as a free man would be over and he'd live out the rest of his days in jail. It was too risky.

No, he definitely couldn't allow that to happen...

He saw the iron key on the kitchen table, among the scattered content of Mary's bag. Then he looked across at Mary's lifeless body...

The cavern!

It *was* a solution, he thought. It wasn't what he wanted for Mary – she deserved some dignity, especially after all she'd gone through because of him, but she was dead now and all that was left was a carcass. He could take her to the cavern and hide her body with the others. That would solve all his problems. No dead body, no meddling police, no questions. If they asked him if he knew anything, well – he *was* an accomplished liar. He'd think of something...

Wheelan knew he had to act quickly. He remembered having to deal with the youth's body and he knew rigor mortis would set in within hours. Mary would be heavy and awkward enough to drag through the undergrowth without having to contend with that as well. If this was going to be his plan, he'd have to act now.

Before he disposed of the body, he had a phone call to make. He couldn't risk anyone seeing Mary's car in the driveway and it was already gone 6am. He fumbled for the address book in the hall dresser and found the number he wanted. It was one of Morgan's old cronies but he knew he'd do a reliable job.

'It's Wheelan. I need a job doing urgently'. Wheelan waited while the man awoke fully. He was obviously still in bed. 'I want you to steal a car from outside the manse. It's a red Fiat. I'll leave the keys and your money in the car. Torch it – no evidence – you understand?' He heard the man acknowledge his instructions. 'Quickly please – I want it done within the hour. You'll be well paid'.

Wheelan pulled on his walking boots from the kitchen, took Mary's car key off the bunch and grabbed a roll of £50 notes from the drawer in his study. He went out into the cool morning air, a sea breeze gently coming in from the sea. He placed the money and the keys on the driver's seat and quietly closed the door. That was that taken care of, he thought. He looked around furtively; anxious that he might be seen.

It was all clear.

Wheelan made his way around to the back of the chapel and opened the store room door. He bundled up the tarpaulin he'd used to cover the youth just days before and carried it in through the back door of the manse.

He went over to Mary, laying out the tarpaulin next to her. He could drag her on this, he thought. He looked at her lifeless body slumped in his hall. It felt surreal. Mary was actually dead and he was about to hide her body in a decrepit cavern. It didn't seem right. But he had to do it – there was no other way if he was going to escape the questions, the investigation and the inevitable jail sentence.

He pushed his hands beneath her shoulders and under her arms and pulled. Her feet thudded on the last few steps as he lifted her onto the tarpaulin. A few adjustments and she was centred on the tough plastic sheeting, he pulled her twisted leg straight and felt her hip crack. He flinched as he heard the broken bones grating against each other.

Now he'd have to secure her so she wouldn't slip off the tarpaulin. Wheelan started hunting in the kitchen; then remembered there was a long coil of thick rope in the chapel store room. He fetched it and started tying the tarpaulin securely to Mary's dead body. When he reached her head, he stopped.

He looked into her lifeless eyes for the last time...

'I'm so sorry it ended like this, Mary. You deserved so much better'. He gently smoothed her hair back from her face before covering her with the tarpaulin and securing it with rope. He fashioning a rope handle around her chest.

Wheelan dragged Mary by the rope through the hall and into the kitchen. He left her near the back door while he cleaned up the blood at the bottom of the stairs. He couldn't risk it being seen through the hall window.

He went back into the kitchen, pocketed the iron key and took a few antacid tablets. His stomach was giving him pain again. He'd have to get it looked at some time, he thought. But not today...

Wheelan quickly checked outside. Thankfully, there was nobody in sight. He pulled Mary through the back door, dragging her behind him. The body was heavy and Wheelan struggled to keep up the effort it took to get her through the woods and up the hill toward the cavern.

He reached the fence and was forced to stop. How the bloody hell was he going to get her over this obstacle, he thought. He rested for a few minutes, trying to think his way out of it. He could break the fence and drag her through but that would leave tell-tale signs. He'd have to get her over it somehow.

Wheelan braced himself and hauled Mary's upper body into a sitting position, so that she was leaning against the fence. He straightened up to catch his breath. She was a hefty woman. It wasn't going to be easy. He put his arms tightly around her torso and heaved her into a standing position. When the top of the fence was level with her hips, he twisted her around and let go. Her upper body fell heavily as it folded over the wooden rail of the fence. Her face hit the other side with a stomach-churning thud. Wheelan winced. Then, he lifted her legs over and her limp body crumpled into a heap on the ground.

Wheelan caught his breath. This was taking it out of him. His stomach hurt more than ever, but he had to finish the job. He felt a pang of regret. He should have called an ambulance and lived with the consequences. But there was no going back now.

Wheelan climbed the fence and resumed dragging Mary's body to its final resting place. He made easier progress on the pathway that, ironically, Mary herself had beaten through the undergrowth to get to the cavern.

Wheelan reached into his pocket for the key and unlocked the door. It creaked open and the vile stench hit his nostrils hard.

Fuck it, he thought. He'd forgotten the torch. He'd have to feel his way in the dark.

He allowed his eyes to adjust to the gloom of the entrance to the cavern. He gradually got his bearings and tried to remember the layout of the building. Then, he began dragging Mary's body into the cavern to take her place with Morgan's victims. Suddenly, it didn't feel right. Wheelan hadn't anticipated the irony in his plan, but he had to continue...

He cautiously felt his way along the stone wall of the entrance corridor, the dampness creating a slippery, algae-covered surface. Wheelan shuddered. It felt grotesque but he was here now and he had to complete the gristly task.

Barley able to see in the dark, with only the back-light from the entrance to guide him, Wheelan dragged Mary's hefty body further into the cavern. He almost tripped on something. It was hard and flicked onto his foot. He peered down to see what looked like human bones, the shape faintly outlined in the gloom. He touched it again with his boot. It was definitely bone. Dear God; Mary was right. This was evidence that could be used against him if it was ever found. It was a squalid and desolate place.

Wheelan panicked. He left Mary's body where it lay and hastily started to make his way back to the entrance. He had to get out of there...

He fumbled his way back, guided by the stone wall and the tiny slit of daylight ahead. The scurrying sound of rats in the far corner of the cavern repulsed him and spurred him on.

He reached the doorway of the cavern, fumbling for the key. He hastily stepped out and locked the door behind him before making a rapid retreat back to the sanctuary of the manse. The stench of the cavern stayed stubbornly in his nostrils as he took great gulps of fresh air.

Wheelan was breathless and shaken. He hadn't bargained for all this. His heart was pounding and his stomach hurt. He badly needed a drink...

He retraced his steps, climbing the fence and following the rough, overgrown path back to the manse. The exercise was starting to calm him down. He could see Mary's car had gone – at least all the evidence had disappeared.

Wheelan entered the kitchen and kicked off his muddy boots. There in front of him were Mary's things. Her handbag turned upside down, its contents strewn along the length of the table. He pulled up a chair and sat in his usual place. Suddenly, the reality of the situation hit home.

Wheelan felt alone...

He had no one. The one person who cared about him, had looked after him and was always there for him was gone. And it was all thanks to his crass stupidity. He'd been blinded by so many unfounded fears. His selfishness had stood in the way, not only of Mary's happiness but of his own. Now there was no one left to turn to...

He dropped his head into his rough, calloused hands. 'I'm sorry Mary. Really I am'. For once in his life, he felt unremitting remorse for what he had done. He had all but murdered Mary and left her to rot in that putrid, forsaken cavern.

He was a despicable excuse for a human being. He knew that. And he knew he'd have to live with it for the rest of his worthless life.

After long minutes, Wheelan finally pulled himself together and slowly replaced Mary's belongings one by one into the handbag. He savoured the familiar smell of her perfume as he took the bag into his study. He pushed it deep into a drawer and pushed the cavern key in with it. He locked the drawer and tossed the key into a tall vase on the cabinet. He never wanted to see it or be reminded of what he had done ever again.

As more of a distraction than anything else, Wheelan got cleaned up and poured himself a whiskey. It was mid-morning but he didn't give a damn. He needed a drink to steady his nerves and take away the still vivid scene of Mary lying dead in his hallway. It replayed constantly in his mind and he desperately needed peace. More than ever, he just needed the calm sanctuary of his home.

But now Mary would forever be there, lying dead at the bottom of the stairs in his mind's eye.

The manse was eerily quiet, except for the rhythmic ticking of his father's antique clock. It was a rude reminder of how he'd ruined his life – his father would have been horrified at how his son had turned out.

He took a large gulp of his drink and looked through the window to see Katie Halliday waving at him from the driveway. That bloody Doberman was there as well.

Shit, Wheelan thought. She's the last person on Earth I want to see. But it was too late to hide – he'd been spotted. At least the place was clean and any incriminating evidence was squared away.

Wearily, he got up at the sound of the doorbell. Would he ever be allowed to rest, he thought. He would have to put her off...

Katie stood on the doorstep, the ancient dog at her side. He had to put her off. He couldn't face childish chit-chat at the moment. She beamed up at him, her smile lighting up her whole face.

'Not today, Katie, there's a good girl. I'm not feeling too well'. Wheelan wasn't lying. He was feeling like crap and the pain in his stomach was worsening by the minute.

Katie looked dejected but ever cheerful, she said, 'Can I help you Reverend?'

Wheelan just wanted her to go away and leave him to his pain and his ever darkening depression. The only thing that could help him now was the oblivion of his booze.

Katie persisted. She looked concerned. The dog sat dutifully at her side. 'Is Mary here today?'

Wheelan didn't have the patience for this. He snapped at the girl. 'Just go away and leave me alone'.

He gestured to brush her off but his hand accidentally hit her face.

She squealed, clutching her cheek.

Barney lurched forward to protect her.

Wheelan instinctively kicked out at the dog, catching him full in the side of the head.

Barney yelped, backing off in distress. He was shaking his head from the force of the kick.

Wheelan suddenly felt his stomach lurch. He doubled up in agony.

A searing pain shot through his upper abdomen.

He vomited fresh blood before collapsing in the doorway…

Chapter twelve: the truth

After the episode with Mr Ridley, Mike had no option but to stop all prescriptions for bravafloxacin. This new drug had only just come onto the market, fresh from clinical trials and it had barely finished being screened for interactions with other pharmaceuticals. Mike decided it wasn't worth risking more lives. He'd immediately stopped the antibiotic for all the patients on the ward, replacing it with a trusted brand if the patient genuinely needed it for a bacterial infection. Most of the patients came off antibiotics completely since they were unnecessary.

Jenny was relieved. That was one issue sorted out at least but there was still the problem of Isobel. She knew she had to confront Mike about it or she'd go crazy. She felt like her life was crumbling around her and she had to take action soon.

Jenny finished her shift and drove home with a heavy heart. She could put this off no longer. All the way home, she went over and over in her mind what she would say to her husband. Once Katie was in bed and asleep, she would talk to him – she had no choice now...

She pulled up outside the cottage around 8.30pm. She was drained from an eventful shift and emotionally exhausted from the incident at Mrs Baxter's house that morning – not to mention the turmoil of seeing Mike with Isobel.

Mike had arrived home before her to relieve Laura and get Katie to bed but as Jenny opened the front door and went into the hall, she could hear shrieks of laughter and cheers coming from Mike and Katie in the kitchen. Jenny put her bag and her keys on the hall table and made her way into the kitchen, surprised at all the merriment.

She opened the kitchen door and could see that Honey was giving birth to her puppies. Mike and Katie were sat on the floor near Honey's basket. They both looked up, smiles beaming from their faces.

'Mum, come and see. Honey's had three puppies already and there's more on the way'. She was squealing with excitement.

Mike was grinning at his wife. He held a hand out to invite her to join them. Jenny crouched down next to Honey and ran her hand over the Labrador's broad head.

'Oh Honey, you clever girl'. Jenny peered into the basket to see three tiny puppies, all golden yellow, a boy and two girls. They were irresistibly cute as they wriggled around, helplessly.

Mike guided each one to Honey's teats, his big hands gentle and comforting around their plump, warm bodies. 'There you are little fella', he said as he placed the latest one close to Honey. She licked the pup. Mike was smiling and seemed relaxed and happy for the first time in weeks.

Honey looked lovingly at him as if she was thanking him. She looked across at Jenny, the pride of a new mother brimming in her big brown eyes. Jenny stroked her again and kissed her head. It was a magical moment and her troubles momentarily faded into insignificance.

Jenny beamed at Katie. Her little girl was ecstatic – almost beside herself with happiness. She knew they would have to keep at least one of the puppies. Katie would never forgive her parents if they refused her that.

'Barney and Treacle have been banished to the conservatory', Mike said with a grin.

Jenny nodded. The familiar cheeky glint in his eyes was back. She smiled at him. But it was bitter-sweet. Her heart surged with love for her husband – she could barely contemplate life without him – yet she was sad. This 'thing' with Isobel was threatening their marriage. The conversation she'd planned all the way home would have to wait...

'Look Mum, another one's coming!' Katie said, captivated, as Honey was bearing down.

They all urged the Labrador on as she delivered a fourth puppy, this time a black male. They waited with trepidation; then gave a collective sigh of relief as the puppy wriggled and squealed in response to its mother's frantic licking. Mike snuggled it gently between its siblings. Honey was revelling in new motherhood and the extra attention she was getting from the family.

Twenty minutes later, Honey delivered another black puppy. Again, they waited for the pup to breathe and move.

But it was motionless, despite Honey's frantic attempts to revive her precious baby.

'Daddy – do something', Katie shrieked.

Mike had not interfered with the natural process of birth until now but the tiny new-born was clearly in trouble. 'OK, Honey, you need some help there girl', he said reassuringly. He reached out to the pup and cleared the birth sac from around his mouth and face. He grabbed an old towel and rubbed the pup's body briskly and firmly as Honey anxiously licked her baby.

Mercifully, the pup finally took its first breath and wriggled in response to the stimulation.

Everyone sighed with relief.

'Oh, Dad, can we keep that one?' Katie pleaded.

Mike looked at Katie and smiled, 'We'll see', he said.

Katie looked over at her mother. '*Pleeeese* Mum, can we?'

Jenny and Katie both looked at Mike and he gestured defeat, Katie's grin broadening even wider.

'OK, we'll keep that one', Jenny said.

Katie leaned over and kissed Jenny then her father, her utter relief clearly expressed in her face. Father and daughter cuddled up together next to Honey and her puppies, a picture of happiness. Mike looked across at Jenny and smiled.

This was her little family. She loved them and would fight to keep them all together.

Honey groaned in pain as she bore down once again. This time she delivered a golden yellow puppy, a chubby little girl. The pup whimpered almost straight away in response to her mother's licks and Katie reached out and put the pup next to the others. There were six puppies in a row along Honey's abdomen, all eagerly suckling.

Then after ten minutes the final pup was born. This time a golden boy, who took his first breath within moments, responding quickly to Honey's furious licks.

Honey settled down and it became clear that she had delivered all of her little family. Jenny began to clean up her basket and Katie offered the exhausted Labrador a drink of water and some biscuits, which she devoured appreciatively.

'Well, girls, I think this deserves a celebration', Mike said. He stood and went to the refrigerator. He pulled out a bottle of chardonnay for Jenny and himself and some lemonade for Katie. He poured the drinks and they chinked glasses, a resounding ring welcoming the new puppies. 'To Honey and her pups', Mike said.

'To Honey and her pups', Jenny and Katie said in unison.

Jenny sipped the ice cold wine, the sharp taste welcome and refreshing. She looked around at the scene of harmony in the kitchen and decided to forget her troubles for today. There would be another time to confront Mike. For now she wanted to enjoy the contentment of her family – for all she knew, it could be for the last time…

Katie let Barney and Treacle into the kitchen. Barney sat a few feet away from Honey and the pups, eyeing them carefully, while Treacle sniffed and licked his little brood of pups. He was a proud father at last.

It was late when they all fell into bed exhausted, Honey was left to tend to her babies alone in the kitchen, while Barney and Treacle had the rare treat of being allowed to sleep in the sitting room.

+++

The following morning, Jenny awoke to the sound of ambulance sirens. It sounded as if it was coming from the beach. Startled, she got out of bed to check on Katie. Her little girl had a habit of getting up early and going to the beach with Barney.

Mike stirred but stayed in bed, grumbling about the noise outside.

Jenny opened the door to Katie's room. She was gone. She called out to her but there was no reply. Jenny ran downstairs to find Barney missing as well. She felt a rush of adrenaline as she pictured harrowing scenes in her mind's eye – her beautiful daughter could have been hurt.

Or worse...

Memories of Jenny's near death experience flashed through her mind as she panicked for her little girl's safety. As wonderful as the afterlife had been, she didn't want Katie to experience it yet. She had so much life left to live.

Dressed in only her nightdress, dressing gown and slippers, Jenny ran out onto the cliff to scan the area. She was desperate to see Katie unharmed.

As she reached a vantage point just fifty yards from the cottage, she saw an ambulance advance up the slipway from the beach. Her stomach cramped into a tight knot, fearing the worst...

Then as the vehicle reached the top of the slipway; it stopped. The passenger door opened and Katie and Barney stepped down. Katie pushed the door shut and waived as the ambulance picked up speed, the sirens once more blasting out into the still morning air.

Jenny called and waived to Katie and the little girl looked up, waiving back to her mother. She looked alright, Jenny thought, relief beginning to calm her motherly anxiety.

Katie ran up to her mother. Barney was dragging behind, limping slightly.

Jenny caught her daughter in her arms. 'What on earth happened, Katie?' she asked. 'What were you doing in the ambulance?'

Katie explained what had happened at the manse. 'I went to see Reverend Wheelan and he collapsed on the doorstep', she said. 'I did what you said I should do if something like that happened and I rolled him over into the recovery position and called 999. He'd sicked up some blood.'

'You did exactly the right thing, Katie. You're such a clever girl.' Jenny felt proud of her daughter and relived that she wasn't injured.

Barney waddled up to them and Jenny smoothed his head. He looked in pain. Perhaps it was just his arthritis from jumping down from the ambulance, Jenny thought.

Katie frowned and stroked Barney's back.

When they got back to the cottage, Mike was up and standing in the doorway. 'What was all the drama about?' he asked.

Katie explained what had happened and they all went into the kitchen to make breakfast. Katie had taken it all in her stride and settled down to keep Honey and the puppies company. All seven pups seemed healthy and were feeding well. Honey was a contented, if exhausted mother.

Mike made the usual family breakfast, the incident now over.

Barney had limped off to his bed in the sitting room, preferring to be alone, while Treacle sat close to Katie, proudly watching over his new offspring, one eye on potential scraps from the table.

As Jenny calmed down, she felt uneasy that Katie had been to see the Reverend again. He was decidedly creepy and she would need to have a chat with her daughter about him. For now, he was safely away from her in hospital. Jenny wondered what the problem was – perhaps she'd find out when she got to work later that day.

Both she and Mike were home for a few hours before their afternoon shifts. It would be a good opportunity to talk to him. Jenny felt a heavy reluctance to break the magic of the happiness they had experienced the evening before as Honey delivered her puppies; but the issue wasn't going to go away. She had to ask Mike what was going on. She couldn't face another day with so many burning questions on her mind.

Katie was settled in the kitchen with the dogs and Mike had wandered into the conservatory with a mug of tea. Jenny followed him and quietly closed the door behind her.

They were finally alone together. This was her chance…

'Tide's going out', Mike said absently. 'It looks like the wind is picking up'. He was stood gazing at the breath-taking sea view from their conservatory window.

'Yes', Jenny said, hesitant to start the awkward conversation she knew she had to have with her husband.

157

She took a deep breath and launched straight in. 'Mike, I saw you with Isobel the other day'. She waited for a reaction.

Mike turned to face her. He was visibly startled. Her husband searched her face – an unspoken question in his green eyes. He hesitated to speak, fumbling for the right words.

Jenny broke the awkward silence. 'You seemed to be in deep conversation with her in the hospital concourse. Do you want to tell me what that was all about?' Jenny felt her stomach knot with apprehension. Suddenly, she wasn't sure if she was ready to hear the answer.

Mike slowly ran his fingers through his hair, obviously uncomfortable and unsure how to reply.

Jenny knew in that moment that Mike *had* been covering up something. He was obviously keeping a secret from her. She waited in silence for him to explain what had been going on, her legs trembling slightly in anticipation of his confession that he'd been having an affair.

After agonising moments, Mike finally put his mug down on the coffee table. 'OK, Jenny, you deserve an explanation'. He paused before going on, his fingers nervously raking his hair once again.

Jenny had to sit down. Her legs were threatening to give way. She was shaking as she waited for the bombshell that would destroy their lives together.

Mike sat next to her on their enormous white linen sofa but he perched on the edge of the seat, facing her. He was searching for the words to explain what had been going on.

'I know I've been distant and snappy with you lately. I'm sorry – I've had a lot going on and a lot on my mind.' Mike was reluctant to say the words Jenny needed to hear.

Mike continued; he was fumbling, avoiding Jenny's eyes. 'When Dad told me he had terminal cancer, I just felt so helpless. I didn't know what to do. Then Isobel came along'. He stopped.

Jenny felt the knot in her stomach tighten. She knew the confession was only moments away.

'I couldn't stop myself, Jenny. She was offering a solution and I was clutching at straws'. Mike finally looked into his wife's eyes, pleading for forgiveness.

Jenny could hold back the tears no longer. She was devastated – betrayed for a second time by someone she loved. The bitch Isobel had won again. 'How could you do this, Mike!' she sobbed. 'Isobel of all people! You know how much misery she's already caused'. Jenny reached for a tissue to dry her eyes, the tears flowing freely now the truth was coming out.

'I know, Jenny, but she was there and I needed...' his words trailed off. 'I know now it was wrong'. Mike looked away, shame in his eyes.

Jenny blew her nose and dabbed at the tears that streamed down her cheeks. She reached for another tissue. 'I just can't believe you're having an affair with *her*'.

'What?' Mike sounded astonished. 'You think I've been having an affair?'

Jenny nodded, sobbing uncontrollably.

'Oh Jenny' Mike said, 'there's no way I'd have an affair – least of all with Isobel'. He seemed shocked and insulted at the suggestion.

Jenny slowly looked up at him. She saw the truth in his eyes. 'You mean you and her are not...'

'Absolutely not!' Mike cut in, objecting to the accusation. He saw her tears and grabbed his wife, hugging her tightly. 'I love you. I'd never hurt you like that. You mean the world to me – you and Katie.'

Mike stroked her hair and kissed her forehead, pulling her tightly to his broad muscular chest. He rocked her back and forth, comfortingly. 'I can't believe you thought I'd do that to you. Why would I have an affair when I have you?'

Jenny cried with relief as she held her husband tight – the man she loved with all her heart. Whatever was going on, she knew she could cope now, as long as they were together.

Then, finally, Jenny took control of her emotions, relief spreading through her body like the warmth of summer sunshine. She dried her eyes and sat up, looking into Mike's familiar green eyes. He was smiling at her and she knew everything would be resolved.

But what *had* been going on?

Mike anticipated her question before she asked...

'OK, let me explain what's been happening', he held her hand. 'I was worried about Dad, and I'm sorry if I was aloof with you – I was finding it hard to get my head around it all – you know, men and caves and all that sort of thing', he rolled his eyes at the embarrassing truth.

'Anyway; then Isobel came along. You know she's a pharmaceutical rep right?'

Jenny nodded.

'Well, Mike continued, 'she offered me this promising new cancer treatment called capataxel, and all I had to do in return was boost the sales of her company's flagship new drug, bravafloxacin. That's why I was prescribing it so liberally on the ward'. Mike looked away; once more ashamed of what he'd done. 'I'm really sorry I did that now but I was desperate to help Dad at the time. I just didn't consider the implications'.

Jenny was puzzled. 'Wait a minute – what is capataxel? I've never heard of it'.

Mike looked at her again. 'You wouldn't have heard of it in the NHS, it's a very expensive drug to treat cancer and it's not officially available yet as it's still in late clinical trials. It's effectively an experimental drug but it's shown astounding results. Tumours have been responding and shrinking in a matter of weeks. It could be a lifeline for certain cancer patients but will probably be used as a last resort. I thought if I could get Dad to take it, his tumour would become operable and he would at least have a chance'.

Jenny sighed. She could see why Mike was so keen to give it a try. But there were still questions in her mind. 'OK, so how much is it and why did Isobel have to be involved. Couldn't we have found the money?' Jenny asked, wiping away the last of her tears.

'Sweetheart, it's over £100,000 for a single round of treatment. Not even my Dad can afford that without selling the house and as I say, it's not officially available to buy on the market. Isobel's company make the stuff and she has access to as much as we'd ever need –

provided I helped her by prescribing the new antibiotic. It's just some of the sly tactics used by some of the less ethical pharmaceutical company reps like Isobel. I didn't think – I just grabbed the chance. I guess that makes me as bad as her'. His voice trailed off.

'Did Dad agree to it?' Jenny asked, remembering seeing Mike and his father arguing when she'd seen them through the window from John and Martha's garden.

'He did after a heated debate. I managed to persuade him to give it a go for Mum's sake, although he wasn't happy about it. I think we'd all agree it's not fair that it's not available to everyone, but it *is* at an experimental stage yet. There's hope; and with this experiment with Dad, it could help pave the way for other cancer sufferers. With no other viable option, he was happy to be a guinea pig…'

So that's what the argument had been about, Jenny realised. 'Has it worked?'

'Dad's seeing his oncologist at the clinic this week – we'll know then'. Mike watched her intently, waiting for more questions.

Jenny was concerned about her patients. 'OK, so what was going on with the bravafloxacin? Was it the side effects of the drug we saw in those patients?'

Mike cleared his throat. 'After the scare with Mr Ridley, I did some checking and found out that the screening process for drug interactions with bravafloxacin was inadequate. These side effects weren't picked up in the trials. It's likely it had adverse reactions with a certain class of drug like ibuprofen. It'll be taken off the market until that's investigated'.

'Poor Mr Ridley – I hope he'll be OK. He could have died', Jenny said solemnly.

'Yes he could have and that's why it had to stop. Of course, there's no way to tell that it was the drug but it *was* a strange coincidence that couldn't be ignored'. Mike looked embarrassed.

'You were under pressure to help your Dad', Jenny felt sympathy for her husband. He'd done the wrong thing and had acted in haste but he *was* trying to prevent his father from dying.

'I'm afraid this sort of thing is pretty common in medicine', Mike explained. 'Both general practitioners and hospital doctors are targeted all the time by pharmaceutical companies to induce them to sell more drugs. Reps like Isobel are trained to offer sweeteners – whatever they may be – to get doctors to prescribe their drugs rather than those of their competitors. It's not ethical but it happens'.

'Yes and that sort of opportunity suits Isobel down to the ground. She'd sell her own grandmother to make money. I'm sorry but she's a bitch'. Jenny scowled at the sound of the woman's name.

Mike smiled wryly and nodded in agreement. 'Come on, let's see what Katie's up to. We have to get to work before long', he said, glancing at the clock.

Mike and Jenny shared a tender kiss. Jenny was glad she'd broached the subject. She should never have doubted her husband's fidelity but it felt good to have things out in the open. He was a decent man and she loved him more than ever for caring about his father. He'd acted in haste but had put things right when he fully realised the implications.

But there was one more thing Jenny hadn't resolved. She had to clear the air. 'By the way, why have you been late home so much lately? Was it to do with Isobel and the capataxel?'

Mike smiled at her. 'No sweetheart. I've taken on Mr Westland's private patients while he's been away and was saving the extra money for a surprise holiday for us. Now you've spoilt the surprise!'

Jenny suddenly felt foolish for doubting her husband. 'Oh, sorry!' She chuckled. Now everything had fallen neatly into place.

'I'm sorry – I should have told you', Mike said. 'Come on, let's go and see what Katie's up to'.

They made their way to the kitchen and stood in the doorway. They were hand in hand watching their daughter cuddling the puppies, each one in turn. She was talking to them and chatting to Honey in her own endearing, childlike way. Honey was listening intently to every word the little girl was saying, while Treacle was asleep under the table, his fatherly duties abandoned.

Jenny looked up at Mike. She was content and happy again. Her family was the centre of her life and a secure place from which to reach out and experience the world.

For all its ups and downs, she was glad to be alive.

Chapter thirteen: fear

Wheelan regained consciousness to the sound of an ambulance approaching the manse. Katie was at his side. She had moved him into the recovery position.

Wheelan looked up at her and she frowned. Her cheek was red where his hand had caught her.

'Don't tell your mother about this'. His gravelly tone sounded like a threat from Wheelan and Katie seemed to get his meaning. She was a smart child, far older than her seven years.

The ambulance arrived and after a brief assessment, Wheelan was stretchered into the vehicle. A paramedic spoke to Katie for a few minutes, and then her and Barney got into the front seat and were given a lift to the top of the slipway. Her home was just yards away.

Wheelan wearily answered questions as the ambulance sped toward the hospital in town. He had an oxygen mask over his nose and mouth and an intravenous drip had been inserted into a vein in his forearm before they'd set off. His mouth and throat felt revolting, and there was that familiar metallic taste again. He knew it must have been blood, not arsenic he'd increasingly detected over the past few months. He'd been such a fool to ever think that Mary would have poisoned him.

'OK, Reverend?' the paramedic asked. 'You were lucky that little girl was there. You could have choked when you passed out but amazingly; she knew exactly what to do'.

'Yes, her mother is a nurse and her dad is a doctor. She's probably been well trained', Wheelan mumbled through his mask. He managed a thin smile.

'We'll get you to accident and emergency to be assessed. Just hold on there, won't be long'. The paramedic was bracing himself against the side of the ambulance as it lurched around the corners, the ear-splitting sound of the siren blasting out, averting any further conversation. The driver was radioing through that they were on their way.

Wheelan was still in pain and shaken. He'd already had an eventful morning with no sleep the night before.

And now this...

He was becoming anxious, not knowing what was happening to him. This is my punishment for what I did to Mary, he thought...

The ambulance finally screeched to a halt outside A&E. Wheelan was stretchered in to the triage room where a team of medical staff in blue scrubs were waiting. He was transferred onto a treatment couch as the paramedic handed over to the doctor.

'This is Reverend Lucas Wheelan, seventy years old, found vomiting fresh blood before collapsing outside his home. We've administered oxygen and he has an intravenous infusion of saline running. No signs of trauma – possible underlying condition. Sorry, we didn't have time to pass a nasogastric tube'. The paramedic turned to Wheelan, 'they'll take care of you now'. With a parting smile and a wave of his hand, he went off to speak to one of the doctors.

Wheelan turned to see a pretty dark-haired nurse in blue scrubs. She was running intravenous infusion tubing through an electronic pump. She smiled briefly at him.

What the hell was happening, he thought.

Before he could ask, the nurse was gone. Everyone was bustling around, fetching things, wheeling trolleys, adjusting equipment, huddled over medical charts and notes. The atmosphere was intense with bleeping monitors, bright lights and the reek of hospital disinfectant.

The pretty nurse returned, took his blood pressure and held an electronic thermometer in his ear until it bleeped with his temperature reading. She attached leads to his chest and hooked him up to a heart monitor. She explained bluntly that she would have to pass a nasogastric tube down his nose and into his stomach to draw off any blood that was still there. He looked horrified but nodded, not relishing the idea one bit.

The nurse went off to prepare her trolley and returned a few minutes later. She'd put on a plastic apron and deftly snapped on a pair of latex gloves. She smiled and leaned toward him with a length of plastic tubing. 'OK Mr Wheelan, this will be a little uncomfortable for a few seconds. Just swallow a few times when you feel it in your throat'.

Wheelan's eyes watered as she pushed the tubing firmly up his nose and down into his oesophagus. He swallowed hard, feeling the plastic scratch the back of his throat as she threaded more and more of the tubing down until it reached his stomach. No kidding, he thought, this is extremely unpleasant.

The nurse checked the tube was in the correct position before taping the excess to the side of his nose. A long length of it was left hanging from his nostril. He could see it in the corner of his eye like an enormous boil. This was undignified, he thought.

What the hell next. He hated hospitals…

The nurse attached a 50ml syringe to the end of the nasogastric tube and pulled the plunger. The syringe immediately filled with bright red frothy blood and gastric secretions. Wheelan watched, disgusted. No wonder he'd been in so much pain and vomiting profusely.

'There you are,' the nurse said brightly, disconnecting the syringe. 'The doctor will be along to examine you shortly'. With that she disappeared again.

Wheelan felt uneasy. What was going on? One minute he was at home trying to come to terms with the fact that he'd let Mary die and had dumped her body unceremoniously in a cavern – and now he was in a hospital emergency room being prodded and poked, having tubes shoved down his throat. He just wanted to get out of there and go home to lose himself in the bottom of a whiskey bottle.

He turned to see a doctor at his side, a stethoscope slung casually around his neck. He was scribbling in Wheelan's sparse medical notes.

'I just want to take a medical history,' the doctor said without looking up from his writing.

Wheelan felt decidedly uncomfortable. He'd always avoided doctors like the plague.

The doctor finally looked at Wheelan over the rim of his spectacles. 'Now then – would you like to tell me what's been happening?' The doctor stood with his pen poised.

Wheelan took a deep breath. He didn't want to go into all that but since he was there, he reasoned he'd have no choice. He explained to the doctor that he'd been having nausea, pain and vomiting which had steadily got worse over the past few months. He'd noticed blood a couple of times as well. The doctor then asked the inevitable questions about his diet and alcohol consumption. Wheelan had to admit he liked a whiskey now and again but there was no way he was going to admit just how much he drank.

The doctor wrote everything down judiciously. 'OK - so have you had any illnesses or operations in the past?'

Wheelan said he hadn't, apart from a nasty dog bite a few years before that had needed stitches.

The doctor leaned in and peered at the scar which ran the length of his cheek. 'And what about this scar? How did you get this?' The doctor touched the scar with his index finger.

Wheelan pulled back, irritated at being touched. He felt violated. There was no way he could admit how that happened. 'Just an accident many years ago', he lied.

The doctor asked more questions and Wheelan dutifully answered. At least he could honestly say no when he was asked if he took recreational drugs. He might have dealt drugs but he never touched the stuff himself. He'd tried cocaine once but it gave him tremors so he stuck to his whiskey after that. Doing drugs was a mug's game, he thought.

Finally, the doctor finished his interrogations and examined Wheelan. He listened to his heart and lungs then put a cool hand on his upper abdomen and pressed down. Wheelan suddenly recoiled in pain. That bloody hurt, he thought. He couldn't wait to get out of there.

The doctor completed his abdominal examination and again wrote on his notes. 'We're going to have to admit you, I'm afraid. You'll need more tests'.

Wheelan was stunned. He wasn't expecting that. He realised he should have known it was a possibility but it had all happened so fast. He was still reeling from the events that had unfolded with Mary during the night and that same morning. How could he possibly take all this in as well?

'How long will I be in?' Wheelan asked. 'I have to get home'. He suddenly felt an icy blast of panic. He didn't want to be kept in hospital to go through any more of their prodding and jabbing. Why couldn't they leave him alone?

'Not sure at this stage', the doctor said. 'It all depends on the test results. He turned to one of the nurses. 'Let's get him admitted to ward six and we'll need an endoscopy'. With that he strode off.

Wheelan's heart sank. It felt strange and isolating to be in such an alien environment and he didn't like the idea of having to sleep in a ward full of other patients. He'd heard awful things about hospitals and he liked his privacy.

He felt sick again.

He started to retch uncontrollably.

One of the other nurses rushed over to Wheelan just as he vomited fresh blood over the sheets.

He felt feint but heard the doctor shout, 'Let's get him into theatre', before he blacked out again.

Chapter fourteen: under the knife

Laura arrived to take care of Katie while Jenny and Mike went to work. She seemed thrilled to meet the new puppies and Jenny knew Katie and her baby sitter would have an entertaining day together with the dogs.

As usual, Jenny felt a pang of guilt at leaving her daughter – it was always a wrench, especially with the excitement of the pups. She wanted so much to share Katie's enjoyment. Mike and Jenny were both scheduled to work a shift in theatre and Jenny was glad they would have a chance to spend some time together, even though it was at work. They would both travel in Mike's Range Rover and Mike was ready to leave.

'I'll just check on Barney', Jenny said. She hadn't seen him since he'd limped off to his basket in the sitting room earlier that morning. There had been so much going on with the incident with the ambulance and the talk she'd finally had with Mike that poor Barney had been forgotten.

Jenny went into the sitting room to find the old dog still in his bed. She gently stroked his head. 'Are you OK Barney?' The Doberman looked at her, his eyes still bleary from sleep. He lifted his head up slightly. 'You've had an eventful morning – no wonder you're so tired', Jenny said to him.

'Come on Jenny or we'll be late', Mike called from the hall.

'Sorry Barney; got to go. I'll see you later'. She kissed his warm soft head and left him to go back to sleep.

Jenny hugged Katie tight and kissed her cheek. 'Bye sweetheart. Have fun and look after those puppies!'

Jenny climbed up into the 4x4 and Mike drove off. They waved to Katie and Laura and soon they were speeding along the coast road toward the hospital in the next town. Rain was starting to splash onto the windscreen and the sea looked dark from the shadow of cloud cover. The wind had picked up and there were white caps on the waves stretching far out to sea.

'Barney's looking tired out, poor thing', Jenny said.

Mike switched on the windscreen wipers. 'Well, I guess he's getting old now. I know how he feels some days'; he said glancing at Jenny with a cheeky grin.

Jenny smiled back. It was good to see Mike getting back to his old self – she hated it when they didn't talk. Thankfully it was a rare thing. 'I'm glad we had that chat this morning', she said.

'Yes, it's good to clear the air and I feel better now you know what's going on. I hated keeping a secret from you', he glanced across at her. 'I still can't believe you thought I was having an affair – with Isobel of all people'. Mike shook his head in disbelief but now seemed mildly amused by the idea.

Jenny felt foolish. She'd let her emotions run away with her imagination. It just showed how toxic Isobel had been in her life. 'Sorry about that. I should have known you'd never hurt me like that'.

Mike looked at her and smiled. 'You never have to worry about that, Jenny. I love you and Katie and that's enough for me'.

'I love you too', she said.

Mike turned the car into the hospital car park. They managed to park near the entrance and walked through

173

the corridor to the theatre hand in hand. Jenny was smiling. It was hard to believe that only the day before, she was convinced their marriage would be over; but now they were more in love than ever. She was grateful and glad she'd broached the subject.

'I *do* have an active imagination', she thought. Perhaps that's where Katie got her flights of fancy from. Jenny had pushed the incident at Mrs Baxter's house to the back of her mind – she'd had more pressing things to deal with. Now those feelings and images of remembering her past life as Helen were fading. Jenny wanted to leave them firmly in the back of her mind. Whether it was true that she had lived a life as Helen before or not, she couldn't see what relevance it had to her life with Mike and Katie now.

It was best forgotten, she thought.

'OK, see you in theatre', Mike said as they reached the staff changing rooms.

'See you soon', Jenny said as they kissed briefly and went their separate ways.

Mike went into the doctor's changing room and Jenny into the nurse's room at the entrance to the operating theatre department. She changed into blue scrubs and tied her hair back. She smiled at her reflection in the mirror. Life was good again, she thought.

Jenny took the staff handover and checked the afternoon's theatre list. There was the usual mixture of general surgical procedures in Theatre One; gynaecology in Theatre Two; orthopaedics in Theatre Three and cardiothoracics in the new theatre wing. Jenny was scheduled to work as a swab nurse in the gynae theatre. She sighed, feeling disappointed. She'd hoped to be working with Mike in the general surgery theatre. Still – it would be less demanding than getting scrubbed to assist with an operation and hopefully, she would see him briefly in the coffee room between patients.

Mike waved to her from the other end of the corridor and charmingly blew her a kiss. He had changed into blue scrubs and was headed for the theatre sister's office. Jenny chuckled. She was relieved and happy that they'd sorted things out.

Suddenly the doors opened behind her and a patient was being wheeled into the anaesthetic room. Time for work, Jenny thought as she headed into Theatre Two. She pushed the plastic doors open and strode across to Marie, the scrub nurse who was preparing a trolley for a D&C, a minor gynaecological procedure.

'Want to count the swabs?' Jenny asked.

'Sure, just give me a minute to open these packs', Marie said. 'How are you, Jenny – has that dog of yours had her pups yet?' The gowned nurse ripped open a sterile pack of white gauze swabs.

'Fine thanks, Marie and yes, Honey had her puppies last night. She had seven and they're all gorgeous – a mixture of black and golden labs. Katie is determined to keep one and we've relented. They *are* very cute', Jenny said.

The two nurses were about to count the swabs in preparation for the operation when the door burst open and the theatre sister called over to Jenny.

'Sorry Jenny, change of plan. Could you scrub in for Theatre One please – we have an emergency laparotomy on its way down from A&E. Apparently collapsed and vomiting blood', sister seemed to be in a tearing hurry.

'On my way', Jenny said as she hastily made her way to the general surgical theatre's scrub room. She was pleased at the sudden change of plan. She'd be working with her husband after all.

When she arrived, Mike was already scrubbing. A junior nurse stood waiting to offer him his surgical gown and gloves.

'Hello, sweetheart – nice to see you!' Mike said smiling at her.

'Yes you too', Jenny said as she grabbed a brush and began lathering antiseptic scrub onto her hands and forearms. 'What's the story here?'

'They've bumped my first patient for this emergency laparotomy. The patient collapsed after vomiting blood in A&E. We'll find out more when we get in there'. Mike rinsed his arms and turned the tap off with his elbow. He shook the excess water droplets into the stainless steel sink and wiped his hands and forearms with a sterile paper towel.

'See you in a minute', he said as he plunged his arms into a sterile theatre gown a nurse was holding out for him. She dodged around the back of the surgeon and tied his gown while Mike snapped on a pair of latex gloves.

Jenny scrubbed furiously then also gowned and gloved. She practically ran into the theatre.

'It's OK, no rush', Mike said. They're still on their way down. He was stood waiting, his gloved fingers clasped to his chest.

A gowned and gloved nurse was preparing a standard laparotomy tray. 'Nearly ready for you, Jenny. Do you want to take over?'

Jenny nodded and continued to sort and check the instruments. Mike wandered over. Jenny glanced up and smiled at him behind her mask. His eyes creased at the corners as he smiled back. This was more like it, Jenny thought. She loved the atmosphere of a busy theatre and she loved watching her husband work.

Jenny finished organising her trolley and stood waiting for the patient. Mike was pacing slowly around the room, glancing up at the clock periodically.

Tom Clarke, a junior doctor appeared, gowned and gloved, ready to assist Mike with the operation.

A few minutes later, in a burst of activity, the patient was wheeled into the anaesthetic room.

Through the glass pane in the door, Jenny could see the anaesthetist and his assistant performing rapid induction anaesthesia. The patient was intubated and the usual paraphernalia of oxygen and cardiac monitors were attached. A theatre orderly put up a new bag of fluid on his intravenous infusion. A nurse aspirated the patient's nasogastric tube, obtaining a syringe full of dirty red fluid.

Jenny couldn't see the patient's face clearly, although she caught a brief glimpse. He looked familiar…

Soon, the orderlies wheeled the patient into theatre and transferred him onto the operating table. He was placed on his back in the supine position with his arms, on extensions, abducted at right angles to his body. One of the theatre orderlies painted the man's naked abdomen with a sickly brown iodine mixture, while another grabbed a set of green sterile drapes. The two orderlies deftly covered the patient with the drapes and adjusted the operating room lights to illuminate an exposed area of the patient's upper abdomen.

Jenny could see the man's face now behind the endotracheal tubing that was being attached to the anaesthetic machine.

It was the Reverend Lucas Wheelan.

Jenny shuddered at the sight of the old scar running the length of his cheek. Somehow it always made her feel anxious. Jenny knew it was ridiculous. As a nurse, she was used to seeing a variety of scars and wounds and none of them bothered her but Wheelan's scar seemed to have some sort of inexplicable significance.

Jenny wheeled her instrument trolley next to the operating table and attached the diathermy. He had been in the ambulance that morning, she remembered, after Katie had bravely helped him. Now *she* had the dubious pleasure of looking after him. She wasn't sure she was ready for this. He still gave her the creeps but at least she didn't have to speak to him while he was anesthetised, she thought wryly.

Mike had been speaking to the accident and emergency nurse that had accompanied the Reverend to theatre. Once he'd finished taking the brief handover, he strode over to his patient.

'OK, so we have the Reverend Wheelan here. Collapsed at home – and rescued by our lovely daughter'. He added proudly, nodding across to Jenny. 'He's been complaining of stomach pain for some time and has been vomiting blood. Apparently there was no time for a CT scan or an endoscopy; he was vomiting blood profusely so they got him to us 'stat' for an exploratory laparotomy. There's some blood cross-matched if someone would kindly fetch one unit from the lab'. Mike glanced at the nurse that was standing alongside him and she scurried off to get the blood.

The junior doctor moved closer to the operating table.

'Ready Tom?' Mike asked.

'Yes, of course', the doctor was keen to make a start.

Mike looked at the anaesthetist, 'OK your end?' he asked.

'Yeah – go ahead, we're good to go'.

Jenny anticipated Mike's laparotomy procedure and picked up the scalpel. The rhythmic sound of the ventilator was conspicuous as the mood in theatre became sombre. Everyone began to focus on the operation at hand.

'OK, let's do a vertical midline incision on the upper abdomen and see what's going on here'. Mike said.

Jenny handed him the scalpel and offered a swab to the junior doctor. He took it and stood poised and ready to mop blood from the incision.

Mike took the scalpel and sliced deeply into Wheelan's flesh. The incision began at the top of his abdomen at the xiphosternum and extended right down to the umbilicus. The surgeon then plunged the knife into the incision again and deepened the cut into the yellow subcutaneous fat. He carefully returned the knife to Jenny. The junior doctor dabbed at small droplets of blood oozing from the tissue.

Jenny handed Mike the diathermy. 'It's set to coagulation', she affirmed.

Mike began sealing off the bleeding blood vessels, clouds of acrid smoke rising up from the open wound. Jenny detested the cloying smell of burning flesh as it stung the back of her throat.

Mike identified the midline of the linea alba; a glistening white layer beneath the subcutaneous tissue. 'Large Mayo scissors', he said, his hand outstretched for the instrument.

Jenny quickly handed him the scissors and he began to carefully open the layer to reveal the pre-peritoneal fat. 'Two straight artery forceps please'.

Jenny handed him the forceps, one at a time, anticipating his preferred surgical methods. She enjoyed working with Mike and was familiar with his techniques.

Mike took the forceps one by one and cautiously picked up the peritoneum, placing the instruments close to one another. Deftly, he snipped the peritoneum between the forceps, unclipped them and extended the incision. Within seconds, the surgeon had skilfully exposed the abdominal organs. They were glistening and wet, the dark red of Wheelan's liver protruding through the open wound.

Jenny handed Mike two retractors and replaced the bloodied Mayo scissors and artery forceps on her trolley. Mike positioned the retractors and handed them to the junior doctor who stretched the incision open to reveal more of the viscera.

Mike's gloved hand reached into Wheelan's abdomen and pulled out the omentum, a fatty layer of visceral fat covering the organs. 'Looks like we have multiple omental deposits', Mike said, pointing out several small lumps embedded in the tissue. He pushed it aside and plunged his hand deeper into the abdomen. He lifted out the stomach.

'Here's the problem. We have a large carcinoma in the fundus of the stomach', Mike said. 'Looks like the primary tumour but he's definitely got metastases. Stage four I would say'. Mike began inspecting the neighbouring organs for further tumours.

The anaesthetist leaned over the top of Wheelan's head to get a view of the tumour. 'Oh dear, stomach cancer – that looks nasty', he said. He checked the unit of blood carefully with the nurse before starting the transfusion.

'Liver looks a bit dodgy too', Mike said smoothing a hand over the fatty-looking organ. He looked over at Jenny. 'Is this the drunk that nearly ran us off the road the other day?'

'Yes, I'm afraid it is', Jenny said, remembering the near crash.

'Not so clever now is he!' Mike said as his gloved hand glided over Wheelan's spleen.

Jenny recalled the darkness in Wheelan's eyes as he'd careered toward them on the road that day. She felt a shiver of revulsion course through the very core of her. He was an absolute creep, she thought. To think her daughter had visited him in all innocence. Perhaps it was really Mary that Katie had taken a liking to. The housekeeper seemed a decent sort, but there was no way she would let Katie near Wheelan again, even though she may well have saved his life that morning.

Mike was examining Wheelan's duodenum and small bowel. 'Well,' he said, 'I'm sorry to say this is completely inoperable. The stomach tumour is certainly too large to excise and there are a lot of small metastases. We're looking at palliative care here'.

Curious, the anaesthetist stood and leaned across Wheelan once again. 'I agree, Mike, not much you can do with that'. He checked the patient's monitor and sat to update his notes.

Jenny and Mike looked at one another. It was a poignant reminder that Mike's father also had inoperable cancer. Mike shook his head. Another life would be lost prematurely. He didn't much care for the Reverend – he'd never had much to do with him – but his personal feelings would never deliberately compromise the medical care he gave a patient. He would have helped Wheelan if it had been at all possible.

'I'll get a biopsy but I'm going to have to close up', Mike said. 'There's nothing I can do'.

Jenny knew he would be thinking about his father and her heart sank. She only hoped that surgery was now possible for him. They would know soon. Even though it had been wrong of Mike to take the bribe from Isobel, the deed was already done. She couldn't help feeling uncomfortable about it though.

The swab nurse offered an open sample pot and Mike snipped off a slither of the tumour and dropped it in with metal forceps. It was a foregone conclusion the lab would confirm it was malignant.

'OK, let's close', Mike said as he replaced Wheelan's abdominal organs into their correct position.

'Do you want a drain?' Jenny asked.

'No, I don't think we need one here. Thanks Jenny'. Mike removed the retractors and the skin and fatty tissue rebounded into place over the organs.

Jenny took the retractors from him, replacing them on her trolley. 'Let's check swabs and instruments', she called to the swab nurse.

Jenny and the nurse counted swabs, abdominal mops, needles and instruments and the count tallied. She handed Mike some catgut for the closure and a small pair of scissors to the junior doctor.

Mike took the needle and began suturing the abdominal wall, the junior doctor snipping the catgut after every stitch was tied. She could see the sadness in her husband's eyes. Life could be harsh, she thought.

The rhythmic whooshing of the ventilator was the predominant sound in the room as the doctors focused on closing the excision, lost in their own thoughts. Jenny glanced at Wheelan's haggard face as he lay on the operating table. She was macabrely drawn to him. Why did she react to the Reverend so viscerally? Perhaps it was the scar or the menacing expression in his grey eyes that made her feel anxious and uncomfortable, yet Jenny sensed it went much deeper than that. It was as if there was more to their association than just the superficial encounters they'd had as neighbours in the same village. Jenny was convinced there must be a psychological connection for him to have such an effect on her. Was it something to do with the chapel? She'd never been a churchgoer but she *had* felt the need to go to Wheelan's particular chapel – that was until Katie had been born. It was strange that once she had her daughter safe and sound in her arms, she suddenly found the chapel and Wheelan repugnant. Something about him was intriguing yet repelling her…

Mike cleared his throat. He was waiting for another length of catgut.

Jenny had been lost in thought. She quickly handed him another suture from her trolley and watched as he deftly sutured Wheelan's subcutaneous fat layer back together. Then she handed Mike the curved needle with the silk for final skin closure.

The surgeon bit deeply into the skin with the needle and expertly tied each suture, the junior doctor on hand to snip the silk. It was always disappointing when nothing could be done to help a patient and the atmosphere in the theatre had become even more solemn.

'OK, that's it', Mike announced when he'd finished suturing the wound. 'Can I leave you to apply the dressing, Jenny? I could murder a coffee and I'll give Dad a call'. He'd obviously been feeling the pathos of the situation and was keen to check on his father.

'Sure, no problem', Jenny said. 'Give him my love and tell him about the puppies – we didn't get time yesterday. It might cheer him up a bit'.

Mike nodded his agreement as he snapped off his gloves, removed his gown and headed for the scrub room exit.

Jenny cleaned the wound and applied a transparent adhesive dressing as the anaesthetist began to bring Wheelan out of the anaesthetic. The orderlies released his arms from the extensions and transferred him onto a theatre trolley. Jenny watched as they wheeled him away to the recovery room.

She wished she could figure out what it was about him that she found so disturbing...

Jenny turned to focus on the task at hand. They had a full theatre list still to complete before the end of her shift. She cleared her laparotomy trolley and put it into the dirty area to be cleaned and autoclaved. She snapped off her gloves and gratefully removed her theatre gown. She was hot under the intense theatre lights and badly needed a few minutes to herself. Wheelan had managed to make her feel anxious and emotionally drained – even though he'd been anaesthetised. It was if his very presence made her uneasy.

Jenny tried to shake off any further thoughts of Wheelan as she made for the nurse's changing room – she had more important things to occupy her mind with. She would make her usual call and see if Katie was alright and grab a quick coffee while theatre was being prepped for the next patient.

Jenny opened her locker and reached for her phone. Laura had left a voice message. Jenny listened nervously; worried that something had happened to Katie. It wasn't like Laura to call her unless it was important.

'Jenny, I'm sorry to call you at work', Laura's voice was carefully measured. 'Katie's OK but she's very upset. I thought I ought to let you know. Barney doesn't seem very well and I can't seem to calm Katie down at all. She's convinced he's really sick. I'm going to get him to the vet and I'll call you later to let you know what he says'.

Jenny was concerned. Barney had seemed quiet that morning since Katie had returned from Wheelan's house in the ambulance. She'd been so preoccupied with talking to Mike and getting to work, she hadn't paid Barney nearly enough attention. Jenny felt guilty. Katie was upset, Barney wasn't well and she was in work again, leaving a babysitter to sort things out. Jenny felt the familiar feeling of being torn between responsibilities. Whatever she did and wherever she was, she had the feeling she should be somewhere else. Right now she should be with her daughter.

Jenny dialled Laura's number but it went straight to voicemail. Perhaps she was driving to the vet's. Jenny left a brief message asking Laura to let her know immediately when there was any news.

She just wanted to go home.

Jenny sneaked the phone into her pocket on 'vibrate only'. Staff were not permitted to take phones into theatre but this was important. She had to know what was happening. She left the changing room and went to find Mike in the staff room. He was sat with a coffee finishing up a call to his father.

'Dad's feeling a lot better, thank God. He's in clinic tomorrow so we'll have more news then. He's looking forward to seeing the pups', Mike said, a smile back on his face.

'That's good', Jenny said. She took a deep breath. 'Mike, I've just had a message from Laura – Barney's not well and Katie is very upset. They're on their way to the vet'.

Mike put his coffee down and stood to speak to Jenny. 'Oh no – what's the matter with Barney?'

'I don't know. She didn't say and I can't get a call through to her. She'll let me know when there's news'. Jenny fought the tears that were welling up.

Mike hugged her. 'Try not to worry. It might not be anything serious. You know what a drama queen Katie can be'.

Jenny wrapped her arms around her husband and held on tight. She just wished they could both be with Katie and the dogs.

'I should go home', Jenny said.

Mike pulled her away from him and stooped to look directly into her eyes. 'Look – just wait a bit and see what Laura says. You can't just go home. You're needed here'.

She knew he was right but she couldn't help worrying. Her little girl needed her and so did Barney. She felt like cancelling all her shifts for the next week.

Mike handed her a tissue. 'Why don't you let someone else scrub in for the next op and you can get Laura's message when it comes. I'll clear it with sister'.

Jenny nodded. 'OK that would be a help. I'll be a runner for Theatre One and Two. I think I can manage that. I'm just so worried'. Jenny knew she wouldn't have the focus required to scrub in for an operation.

'Right – now stop worrying and wait and see what Laura has to say. OK?' Mike's voice was firm but his eyes were gentle and caring.

'OK, I know you're right. I just feel like I should be at home', Jenny said, drying her eyes.

'You're just being a good mum', Mike said, ushering her toward the door, 'but you're a good nurse too. Laura can cope for a few hours'.

Mike spoke to the theatre sister and she agreed that Jenny could step back from scrubbing in while she waited for news. The next hour dragged by as Jenny tried to focus on her work. She was fetching sutures, bags of intravenous fluids, opening sterile instruments onto trolleys and setting up equipment. She was glad to be busy but without the usual intense concentration.

The wait for Laura's call was agonising.

Finally, Jenny felt her phone vibrate in her pocket and she slipped out of theatre signalling to one of the orderlies to cover for her. 'Laura? Is everything OK?' Jenny asked intently.

'Everything is okay, Jenny', Laura sounded calm; 'the vet said couldn't find anything obviously wrong with Barney. It could be that his arthritis has got worse. Anyway, he said to keep him quiet and comfortable and to go back if you're worried. He's given us some painkillers'.

Jenny sighed with relief. 'Thank goodness. Maybe he just walked too far this morning. How is my darling little Katie?'

'She's fine now. She was beside herself earlier but now the vet has seen Barney, she's calmed down. Sorry I worried you earlier'. Laura said.

'That's alright, I'm glad you told me. Can I have a word with Katie?' Jenny heard Laura hand Katie the phone.

'Hi Mum. We're taking Barney home for a rest and I'm going to give him his favourite treats'.

Katie's voice calmed Jenny's concerns. 'That's good sweetheart. I was worried about you all. I'll be home in a few hours'. Jenny still wished she could drop everything there and then and to be with her family.

'OK Mum. I'll look after Barney and the puppies'.

Jenny said her goodbye's and hung up. She was relieved it was nothing serious. Now she could focus on her work and get through the shift.

She went into Theatre One where Mike was just starting a routine hernia operation. She walked over to her husband, careful to avoid touching the sterile field. 'Panic over', she said, 'the vet thinks it's just his arthritis and Katie has calmed down'.

Mike smiled at her beneath his mask, his eyes creasing deeply at the corners. 'That's great news – nothing to worry about then'.

Jenny returned the smile before she went into Theatre Two to help with a hysterectomy patient that was about to be wheeled in.

Jenny had to pass the recovery room on her way. She looked in to see Wheelan awake from the anaesthetic and watching her as he lay on his trolley.

Jenny suddenly felt utterly repulsed by him – his scarred cheek and the menacing blackness in his eyes.

She would be working on the surgical ward the next day and she knew he would be there. She hoped she wouldn't have to deal with him.

Now more than anything she wanted to get home...

Chapter fifteen: bombshell

Wheelan woke in the recovery room; a nurse was checking his blood infusion. The image of her was blurred and he struggled to focus. He felt woozy and his throat was sore from the endotracheal tube. His senses were filled with the nauseous smell of anaesthetic. Wheelan moved his hand to his abdomen – it felt tender and painful. It was only then he fully realised he'd had a surgical operation.

'What happened?' he asked the nurse, falteringly. His voice was hoarse.

'You rest now. They'll explain everything when you get back to the ward'. She smiled and gave a reassuring touch on his arm before going off to see to another patient.

Wheelan felt numb. It was all so sudden. He stared through the door of the recovery room, the bustle of a busy department a strange but welcome distraction. He felt exhausted and badly needed to sleep. He would just have to make sense of it all later.

Then he saw her.

It was Jenny Halliday, the woman from the village. She was glaring at him almost accusingly. Had Katie said anything to her about his outburst? He tried to focus on her, trying to read her expression.

But then she was gone. She had disappeared into the bustle of the hospital.

He could fight his weariness no longer and Wheelan fell into a deep, dreamless sleep…

+++

When he woke again, he was on the ward. Sunlight was streaming in through the window. It was morning. He must have slept right through the previous evening and night.

As he tried to shake off the bleariness of sleep, Wheelan took in his surroundings. Opposite him was a young man listening to music through headphones. A curtain was drawn around the bed next to him and diagonally opposite was an empty bed. He could hear the sounds of the nurses working; trolleys clattering and people talking. Still there was the all-pervading reek of hospital disinfectant along with the fading odour of anaesthetic. He looked down at his body to see the dressing on his abdomen; an alarmingly big wound ran vertically along the length of his upper abdomen, the sutures pulling painfully. He still had the nasogastric tubing hanging from his nose and an intravenous infusion; now giving him clear fluid. Now there was also a syringe pump making occasional whirring noises as it pumped analgesia into his vein.

Wheelan sighed. He couldn't fathom why this was happening to him. He knew he hadn't been feeling well for the past few months but he didn't think he'd end up having surgery.

He lay in his bed contemplating his new situation but his thoughts were interrupted when a doctor accompanied by a petite young nurse came to his bedside.

The doctor cleared his throat before he spoke. 'Reverend Wheelan, I'm afraid I have some bad news for you'. He hesitated a moment before going on. 'Mr Halliday found a large tumour in your stomach. I'm afraid you have cancer'. The doctor paused.

Fucking hell, Wheelan thought – why not get to the point! He felt the shock run icy cold through his veins. 'Cancer?' He could barely believe what he was hearing. 'But you've got rid of it, haven't you. Surely that's what the operation was for'.

The doctor shook his head solemnly. 'I'm sorry but it was inoperable. You have an advanced adenocarcinoma. It looks quite aggressive and has already spread to part of your liver and spleen. Your cancer is at stage four. I'm so sorry; there was nothing we could do'.

The nurse gently held his hand.

Wheelan squeezed the nurse's tiny hand as his mouth gaped uselessly, not knowing how to react. Advanced cancer and nothing they could do. How could that possibly be? He hadn't seen that coming. He was stunned. Did this mean he was going to die?

Moments later Wheelan managed to speak. 'How long have I got?'

The doctor hesitated again before delivering the bad news. 'A few months at most, I'm afraid'.

Wheelan stared at the doctor aghast and then looked up at the nurse for conformation. She nodded sympathetically. Surely this was a mistake. It couldn't be true, he thought. He wanted them to tell him they had mixed him up with someone else but he could see from their expression that what the doctor had told him *was* the truth.

Wheelan felt desperate to get rid of this menacing thing that was growing inside him. 'But there must be something you can do. Can't you treat it, cut it out or give me chemotherapy or something?'

The doctor slowly shook his head once again. 'We can treat your symptoms as necessary but there is no cure. I'm very sorry'.

'But what about drugs? Experimental drugs – anything. I'll do anything to get rid of it'. Wheelan was clutching at any means of ridding himself of this dreaded disease. It was a malevolent parasite eating away at his life.

The doctor thought for a moment, looked at the nurse then back to Wheelan and said. 'No, I'm sorry, there's nothing we could offer you that would help. I don't want to raise your hopes. You have terminal cancer and you will have to come to terms with the fact that you are going to die. We will keep you as comfortable as we can and there will be lots of help and support available'. The doctor smiled benignly and wandered off.

For God's sake! Wheelan leaned back on his pillow, completely stunned. This is totally unbelievable, he thought.

The nurse patted his hand. 'Is there anyone we can call for you?' She asked.

Wheelan shook his head and the nurse wandered off to attend to another patient. It suddenly struck him like a thunderbolt that he had absolutely no one to turn to. No family, no friends and now, no Mary. He was completely alone in this unfamiliar place with nobody he could confide in, nobody that would truly understand what he was going through.

Nobody cared about him.

Nobody loved him...

He badly wanted to hear Mary's voice. He longed to see her walk through the door, smiling at him as she always had. He ached for her to sit with him, comforting him. She was the only one who had ever cared.

And now she was gone...

He couldn't imagine how he was going to cope. What would happen to him? Would he ever feel normal again? Would he be able to eat again? Would he have to give up his whiskey? Wheelan had so many questions running through his mind but all he could feel was numbness and utter shock.

He wished he could rewind the past few months and go back to the way things were before – before he'd killed the youth. He longed for his normal routine. He wanted Mary to be there to take care of him, to cook and clean for him, to mother him as she always had. He ached to hear her gossip, to smell her perfume and marvel at her bright red lipstick. But she was dead. She was never coming back.

Wheelan felt more vulnerable than he'd ever felt in his life. And more afraid...

He was going to die and he was terrified. There was no time to put his life in order. He could be dead within months – weeks even.

The nurse returned to his bedside. 'Are you alright, Reverend?' She asked kindly.

'Still in shock', was all he could manage.

She smiled. 'It's good that you have your faith'.

Wheelan felt the irony. If only she knew, he thought.

If only she knew...

Chapter sixteen: a reprieve

Jenny arrived at the hospital an hour before her afternoon shift on the surgical ward. It was the day of John's clinic appointment with the oncologist and she was anxious to know how he was getting on. Martha, as always, was at his side and Mike was meeting them all there. He'd been out of the house and at work since dawn, having been called in to an emergency. Jenny would be glad when Mr Westland returned to relieve Mike of the extra responsibility.

Jenny made her way to the oncology department to find Mike pacing the corridor. His face brightened when he saw her. 'Hi sweetheart – they're still in there with the oncologist'. He bent to kiss her.

Jenny could sense Mike's concern. It had been a worrying time and he'd put his career on the line to try to save his father. Whether it had been right or wrong, she understood her husband's motivations. She slipped her hand into his. 'Let's hope the capataxel has worked its magic', Jenny whispered.

'Yes, I hope so', Mike said, squeezing her hand.

The door of the consulting room swung open and Martha stepped out, her face beaming. John followed, relief etched deeply into his face.

They hurried over to greet them.

'What did he say?' Mike asked; eager to hear the news.

'The tumour has shrunk – they can operate', John said. He was shaking with relief as Mike grabbed him in a powerful bear hug.

'Oh Dad, it's wonderful. Thank God', Mike said.

Martha hugged Jenny. 'Such wonderful good news isn't it!' she said, tears of joy in her eyes.

'Yes, absolutely – I'm so happy for you', Jenny was thrilled. It felt like a miracle.

They walked together to the hospital lobby. 'A coffee to celebrate?' Jenny asked.

'I could do with something stronger', John said jokily, 'but yes why not'.

They found a table and sat with their coffees, chatting excitedly now the future looked a whole lot brighter.

'So, Dad, when is the op?' Mike asked.

'Tomorrow. We're going to strike while the tumour is operable. It's all down to the capataxel. I don't think I'd have much longer if it hadn't been for that. Thanks son. I'm glad you talked me into it'. John said.

'It could turn out to be a miracle drug to fight cancer', Mike said. He was beaming at his father.

'Yes maybe it will. Let's hope it will be sensibly priced and available for everyone', John said.

They all nodded in agreement.

John continued. 'I'm going to stop taking it now though. It has to clear my system before surgery. I won't be needing it anymore'. He was determinedly positive.

Relieved and excited, they chatted about the puppies and Katie while they finished their drinks. Jenny glanced at her watch. 'I have to get to the ward, I'm afraid. I can't be late again', Jenny kissed John and Martha in turn, 'I'm so happy', she said.

'I'll walk with you', Mike said, 'I have to get back to work too'.

He said his goodbyes to his parents and Jenny and Mike headed for the surgical ward.

Mike was grinning broadly. 'Brilliant news isn't it? Although I'm grateful; now I can tell Isobel where to go with her bloody bribes'.

Jenny agreed. It would be good to get Isobel out of their lives.

They reached the ward and Mike went off to check on a patient he'd seen earlier. Jenny went to change into a set of scrubs and take the staff handover. She was dreading being asked to look after Wheelan when the nurses were allocated their patients for the shift. Her mind was racing with excuses as to why she couldn't nurse him but none of them sounded convincing.

Finally the handover was completed and thankfully the Reverend wasn't on her list of patients, although she would have to attend to him briefly at various points during the shift.

Relieved, Jenny started with her medicine round as usual. Another staff nurse accompanied her. Each patient she went to brought her closer to Wheelan and she began to feel an increasing apprehension in the pit of her stomach. She had to try to control her feelings. He was just another patient, she reasoned – just give him his drugs and move on. Keep a professional facade, she kept telling herself.

By the time she reached Wheelan's bed, her heart was racing…

+++

Wheelan wasn't ready to die.

This had all come as a shock and he hadn't been able to think it through. He wanted to go home and sit in his armchair by the window. He wanted to see the sea again and listen to the soothing sounds of his father's clock. He was irritated at being around other people all the time. His ears were ringing constantly with the sound of trolleys, medical equipment bleeping and people talking. There was no peace. No interlude to get his mind straight.

He had to get home…

He called one of the nurses over to him. 'I really have to get home now.' Wheelan said.

'You're not ready yet, Reverend. You need to stay in at least a few more days. We have to organise some care for you at home and you have to see the cancer nurse'. She smiled at him.

'No wait', he said, grabbing her hand, 'I *have* to go home. I want to discharge myself'. His eyes were imploring her.

'OK, please calm down. Let me at least get the doctor to check you over. Will you wait for that?' She said.

'Alright but I want to be out of here by this afternoon'. Wheelan said firmly. He had made up his mind.

He tried to sit up. He was stiff and his wound was painful but he just had to get out of the hospital. He felt the nasogastric tube hanging from his nose. I'm going to get rid of this for a start, he thought. He peeled the sticky tape from his nostril that was holding the tube in place. Once it was off, he gently pulled. The movement of the plastic at the back of his throat was making him gag but he kept pulling until the tube was out. A thick blob of mucus splattered onto the sheet.

'I don't think you should be doing that', the young man in the opposite bed was saying.

Wheelan glared at him, as he began peeling off the tape that was keeping his intravenous drip in the vein in his arm. Mind your own bloody business, Wheelan thought. This is coming out too.

He pulled the cannula of the drip from his arm. Blood and fluid spurted over the white cotton sheets and down his hospital gown. He grabbed a corner of the sheet to try to stem the flow but his arm was bleeding profusely.

He looked up to see Jenny Halliday at the foot of his bed. Great, that's all I need, he thought...

+++

As she approached his bed, Jenny saw Wheelan pull out the cannula on his IVI. She quickly closed the drug trolley, locked it and pocketed the keys before going to help. She didn't like the man one bit but her nursing instincts took over and she knew she had to apply firm pressure to the bleeding vein.

'I'll get some sterile swabs', the other staff nurse said as she hurried off to the treatment room store cupboard.

Jenny pulled a few tissues from a box on another patient's locker and pressed down on Wheelan's bleeding arm. 'Why did you do that?' she asked, avoiding his glaring eyes.

'I have to get home', Wheelan said flatly.

'You're meant to stay in at least a few days', Jenny said. She felt uncomfortable being in such close proximity to the Reverend. It hadn't seemed so bad the day before when he was anesthetised but now he was awake and talking to her and she had no choice but to deal with him.

Wheelan tried to pull away from her and get out of bed. He drew back the sheet to reveal his naked leg, a nasty old scar pitted deeply into his thigh.

Jenny saw it and froze.

Suddenly, a vivid image flashed into her mind. Wheelan was in a cave on the beach and Barney had attacked him. That's what had caused the scar. Barney had been protecting her from this deranged man.

She looked into Wheelan's menacing grey eyes and realised it was a forgotten memory resurfacing in her mind – a memory from before her almost fatal head injury nine years before.

Jenny looked away. She didn't like having to deal with this maniac. No wonder she always felt so awkward and distrustful of him. Her subconscious had been harbouring this disturbing memory all these years. Why had she forgotten the incident? She'd completely blanked the last few days before her head injury. Jenny wondered what else might come to the surface...

'That's a nasty scar', Jenny said, still pressing on Wheelan's bleeding arm. 'That was a dog bite wasn't it –

from my dog, Barney'. Jenny couldn't help herself. She tried to keep her voice level but her head was in turmoil.

Wheelan spun round to glare at her. 'I didn't think you remembered', he said.

'I hadn't until now', Jenny said, glancing again at the hideous contorted scar.

Wheelan covered it up with his hospital gown and dutifully got back onto the bed.

The nurse returned with some sterile swabs. Jenny couldn't wait to get away from the wretched man. No wonder she'd had such misgivings about him over the years. She couldn't fathom him but she knew he was bad news.

Wheelan seemed agitated. 'Please, help me. I have to get home'. He was pleading with her.

Jenny looked at him, unable to answer. She couldn't understand why he had such a powerful effect on her. It didn't make sense. All she could do was to turn and walk away. She would have to let someone else deal with him.

With her hands trembling, she resumed her medicine round. She was battling to stay calm and professional.

Somehow, she knew this wasn't the last of it with the Reverend...

+++

Wheelan felt uncomfortable and embarrassed that Jenny had seen the scar on his thigh. He thought *that* incident was firmly in the past but she'd obviously remembered it. She looked cold and indifferent as she'd walked off. Perhaps it was understandable, he thought.

Shit – why did she have to see that? He had enough to contend with without worrying about ancient history. He was about to die alone and friendless.

The other nurse had stopped the bleeding and dressed his arm. For a few minutes, he stayed on his bed. At least he had managed to rid himself of all those tubes and drips. He was waiting for Jenny and the other nurse to disappear down the ward's corridor so he could get out of there.

Wheelan tentatively got out of bed. His wound hurt like hell. It felt like hot knives were stabbing at his stomach. His muscles were stiff and it was difficult for him to stand up straight but he was determined to discharge himself and get back to the sanctuary of his home.

If it was a sanctuary now…

Mary's pleading face as she lay dying on the hall floor would always be in his mind's eye – a constant reminder that he had mercilessly let her die, desperately unhappy and begging for his help.

If only he could turn back time…

Wheelan dragged the flimsy curtains around his bed, found his clothes in the locker and slowly dressed himself, glad to be out of the crumpled hospital gown he'd been forced to wear since he'd been admitted. It had been humiliating. The stupid thing had barely covered his backside and now Jenny Halliday had seen his scar. If Mary was here, he thought, she'd have brought him pyjamas and slippers and little treats to keep him comfortable. But she was gone and it was his fault. Now he had to suffer the consequences.

He fought against the pain and with a monumental effort; Wheelan was finally dressed and ready to leave. He sat uneasily on the edge of his bed. He'd asked the petite nurse to call a taxi for him. He was determined to get out of there. He'd wait ten minutes for this bloody doctor and if he hadn't come to see him by then, he was off.

As if on cue, the doctor strolled over to Wheelan, his notes, a document and a pen in his hand.

'Nurse tells me you want to discharge yourself?' The doctor sat himself down on the edge of the bed next to Wheelan.

Wheelan shuffled uncomfortably. 'I just have to get home', Wheelan said. 'I have a lot to do and a lot to think about and I can't do it here'.

The doctor nodded. 'Of course; I do understand. You have to put your life in order. I'm afraid you'll have to sign this form to say that you're discharging yourself against medical advice. I do think you should stay in at least a few more days so you can recover from the op and allow us to arrange further care, but if this is what you want…'

Wheelan nodded. Whatever it took, he was going home, back to the manse.

The doctor handed him the discharge form to sign and a prescription for analgesia along with instructions to see his family doctor. Wheelan scribbled his signature and thanked the doctor. He really was grateful to them but it was time for him to be somewhere familiar and comforting.

Wheelan called at the hospital pharmacy and collected a prescription for liquid oral morphine. He shuffled down the corridor, bent like a crippled old man toward the hospital entrance lobby. His wound was sore and his stitches were pulling. He wasn't sure how he was going to cope but he knew he had to get home.

He waited a few minutes until the taxi arrived, sunshine and a fresh breeze on his face at last. He sunk gratefully into the back seat, relieved to be out in the world again. Gratefully, he gave the driver directions back to the manse.

As they meandered through the town traffic, Wheelan watched as people went about their daily lives. It seemed surreal to him. His life had been suddenly devastated by the news that he was terminally ill, yet life still went on around him. Mothers with their children were shopping, men in suits were going about their business; a van driver was delivering parcels. Soon he wouldn't be in this world, yet life would continue for others. It didn't seem fair. Wheelan stared out of the window, bewildered and confused. How the hell could this have happened to him?

Soon the taxi was turning onto the country lane that followed the coastline to the manse, every bump in the road jolted painfully through his body. He managed a bitter sweet smile as he watched the sea, the tide halfway down the beach, a handful of people walking dogs and there were children running and playing in the golden sand. He'd be forced to leave all this and there was nothing he could do to stop it. Ironically, he realised how much this place really meant to him now it was too late.

The taxi slowed and turned right, down the slipway to the beach. This section of the coast became rugged in comparison to the sandy beaches of the west. It was usually deserted. This was how he liked it. They arrived at the manse, gravel crunching beneath the tyres.

Wheelan asked the driver to wait while he got some money to pay his fare. He'd been carted off to hospital with nothing other than the clothes he was in. He struggled to get out of the car, his wound was sore and he was still feeling weak from the operation. He found a key to the front door under a flowerpot, where Mary always left it and went in to find some cash. The place felt strange, smaller somehow and eerily quiet. There was no Mary at the kitchen door to greet him; no delicious cooking smells coming from the oven. Wheelan quickly paid the driver and closed the door on the world as the taxi sped off up the hill.

He was home at last...

Wheelan made himself a strong cup of tea and gently lowered himself into his armchair near the window. He felt safe here. It was his home – had been for most of his life. Yet things were different now. When he sat here last, just a few days before, he'd had the rest of his life ahead of him. Time to put things right perhaps...

But now time was running out. There was no prospect of a future and his life was coming to an end. Wheelan felt an overwhelming sadness.

With a mixture of distress and sorrow, he fully realised how frightened and alone he really was.

A tear spilled down his cheek and soon he was sobbing...

Was this how Mary had felt? Utter heartache for the life they could have had? A life that he'd denied her. Now he felt that too. He could have enjoyed a life filled with happiness and love, yet he'd been afraid. It had all been there for the taking but now it was too late. Mary would never be there again – ever!

It was so final.

He felt her presence everywhere in the house. He had known the sound of her footsteps upstairs, the clattering of dishes in the kitchen, the smell of her perfume and her incessant, yet joyful chatter.

But most of all, he could see her in his mind's eye – she was lying dead at the bottom of his stairs, her cheeks wet with tears.

He sobbed again. This time with sadness and regret at what he'd done. There was no going back. No way to put things right now. Mary was utterly dead; her body lay in the cavern as a stark reminder of his cruel and detestable actions. He hadn't even given her the dignity of a proper funeral. Her children would never know what had happened to their mother and her friends would forever wonder where she was.

Wheelan hated himself and what he had become.

Gradually, he stopped crying, his body spent and exhausted from the rush of overwhelming emotions. He noticed the all-pervading silence in the room. His father's antique clock had stopped ticking. Somehow it felt like his father was letting him know how sickened he was with his son for what he'd become.

Wheelan knew he deserved his father's wrath.

He felt utterly bereft...

Chapter seventeen: life and death

Jenny quietly tiptoed down the stairs. She'd woken early and couldn't settle. Mike had been snoring beside her and Katie was still asleep. She decided to watch the sunrise with a mug of coffee in the conservatory.

She looked in on Barney and Treacle in the sitting room. Treacle opened one eye to acknowledge her then went back to sleep but Barney looked uncomfortable and was making small groaning noises. She went over to him and crouched beside his basket. 'What's the matter Barney, you look sad. Are you OK?' Jenny said, stroking his head. The Doberman looked up at her with soulful brown eyes. He tried to sit up but he was stiff and clearly in pain. 'I think I'll get you to the vet today', Jenny said, 'it won't hurt to get you checked out again'. She leaned in and hugged him, snuggling her face into his soft coat. She loved him dearly and they had been through so much together. She kissed his head. 'Coming to see the pups?' She whispered.

The Doberman struggled out of his basket and followed Jenny into the kitchen. Honey stirred and lifted her head briefly, then went back to sleep. The puppies were lined up along her belly. They were sleeping and twitching as they dreamed their puppy dreams. Jenny gently stroked their warm plump bodies. 'You're a special girl, Honey', she whispered to the Labrador. She adored those puppies and was glad they were keeping at least one. Barney pushed his nose into the basket and gave the pups a lick. He was gentle and placid with them and Honey trusted him implicitly with her babies.

Jenny made her coffee and wandered into the conservatory. Barney was following at her side, still limping slightly. Jenny settled onto the sofa and helped the Doberman get up next to her. She loved their cuddles and everyone knew that she and Barney had a special bond. The cottage was peaceful as Jenny stroked the dog's back, his head resting on her lap. It was his favourite place to be. She watched the sun begin to creep above the horizon; the clouds immersed in the luminescent red and orange of the dawn light. Much as she loved her family, she relished these quiet moments alone with Barney. And with all that had been happening lately, she needed a little time to think; undisturbed.

The Reverend had unsettled her more than she was willing to admit. She wished she could figure out what it was about him that she found so disturbing. He was supposed to be a religious man but she sensed a dark, foreboding side to him. Was it just her or did anyone else see that too, she wondered? She was glad when he'd discharged himself from the ward the day before. Let the stupid old fool struggle at home if he wanted to, she thought. She sympathised with his illness but from what she could see, he was cantankerous and unnecessarily rude to practically everyone he met.

Jenny remembered the scar on Wheelan's leg...

The incident in the cave's that had eluded her for so long came flooding back into her memory. She recalled how he'd stood there glaring at her menacingly in the entrance to the cave and how he'd tried to grab her. She squirmed as she remembered with horror as the scar on Wheelan's cheek had turned bloody and red in her mind's eye. It had seemed so real. Was her subconscious trying to tell her something – maybe to warn her about him? She remembered that Barney had come to her rescue. Why had she forgotten that for so long?

Then there was the creepy vision she'd had at Mrs Baxter's house the other day. She felt as if she actually *was* Helen from her previous life. While she'd been in the old lady's house, she'd experienced powerful emotions and remembered intricate details that she could never have known unless she really had been Helen.

What was happening to her and why was she getting these strange hallucinations? It was alarming. Perhaps the stress of John's illness and the unnecessary worry she'd had over Mike was taking its toll. Maybe it was the aftermath of her head injury or simply the heightened intuition she'd experienced since her near death experience. Perhaps she was simply tapping in to other people's feelings or sensing a potent atmosphere. She wished she could make sense of it all.

Jenny took a sip of her coffee as she pondered the recent events in her life. She felt a peculiar sense of foreboding, as if something was about to happen – something significant – but she couldn't pin it down.

She remembered things that Katie had said in her childlike innocence. Why *had* Katie drawn Mrs Baxter's house so accurately and with so much detail? Katie seemed to know something about the past too with her drawing of a face in the attic window and her comments that it had been Jenny's former home. Was there some connection somewhere? Had Katie inherited her mother's strong intuition? Jenny shivered. It was all quite surreal. Could it be that she really did live a life as Helen and had actually reincarnated into her current life? Jenny remembered reading a book on how young children sometimes remember past lives and how they provide elaborate details that were impossible for them to access, yet can be verified. Perhaps this was happening to Katie. Perhaps she and her daughter had lived a past life together and Katie was triggering past memories for both of them. It was a puzzle she couldn't get her head around.

Barney shuffled slightly, in an effort to get comfortable. Jenny stroked him, his soft coat felt warm and silky beneath her hand. She would call the vet and make an appointment when they opened for the day. She hated to see him unwell, although he had seemed bright enough since Laura had taken him to the vet. He was suffering with his arthritis but she did her best by giving him all the recommended medication and supplements. He was just getting old, she thought, sad to see her spirited Doberman deteriorating.

Jenny remembered the bond she shared with Barney as she'd left her body all those years ago. She was convinced he could see her as she floated above her physical form. He'd looked directly at *her*, rather than at her unconscious body slumped on the ground. Could he remember that too, she wondered? She remembered the experience with the light beings when she'd re-lived special moments from her life with Barney. She'd felt Barney's emotions as clearly as she'd felt her own. It had been a truly profound experience that was impossible to replicate in their physical form. Jenny savoured her memories. It was good for her to stop the relentless hubbub of life occasionally and remember the unconditional love, acceptance and oneness with the universe that existed beyond the everyday life she knew. She wished she could recall more about her experience with the light beings. She struggled to remember everything clearly – especially the being that had interacted with her the most. Jenny found it frustrating.

The sound of voices upstairs cut into Jenny's reverie. Mike and Katie were getting up.

Jenny sighed and watched the sun as it rose above the horizon, the yellow light bursting through the cumulous clouds that drifted slowly across the morning sky. The beach stretched for several miles along the deserted coast, the tide was creeping toward the rocky headland. Gulls were sweeping past the conservatory window, squabbling over food scraps. A new day was just beginning...

'Hello sweetheart', Mike said as he popped his head around the door. 'I wondered where you were'.

'Just had a bit of a restless night, that's all', Jenny said. 'Barney and I have been watching the sunrise – it's beautiful'.

Mike glanced through the window. 'Yes it's gorgeous. I'm making breakfast – want some?'

'Yes that would be nice', Jenny said, 'I'll come and help'.

Mike nodded and went into the kitchen.

Jenny gently manoeuvred herself from beneath Barney's head and stood. She turned and bent to stroke him. 'Have a rest Barney – see you soon'.

The Doberman looked up, his brown eyes searching deeply into hers.

She stroked Barney's head and felt a powerful urge to hug him. She crouched next to him and put her arms around his soft warm body, pulling him close. 'I love you Barney', she whispered as she snuggled into his silky coat.

She held him close for precious moments, feeling a pure and powerful connection with the Doberman. She kissed his face. 'I'll always love you'.

Jenny left Barney to go back to sleep on the sofa and made her way to the kitchen.

Katie bounded down the stairs. 'Hi Mum', she said brightly. Katie skipped into the kitchen, making a beeline for Honey and the puppies. Treacle finally stirred and took up his usual post near the kitchen table, waiting for breakfast titbits.

'I'm going to get Barney to the vet today', Jenny announced. 'He doesn't seem right to me'.

Katie looked at her mother, the shadow of deep concern in her eyes. The little girl didn't comment but she was clearly worried about the Doberman.

'Are you working today Jenny? I've lost track.' Mike said.

'No, I've booked a few days off. I want to spend some time with Katie before she starts back to school'. Jenny looked across to see Katie beaming. She smiled back, glad to finally have some free time to spend with her daughter.

'That's great, Mum!' she said excitedly.

'I'll go into the hospital this afternoon but I have the morning free', Mike said. 'Maybe we could take the dogs to the beach?'

Katie readily agreed. She loved the beach, whatever the weather and today it was perfect.

'I think I will try and call the vet', Jenny said, 'you two go and I'll catch up with you later'. Jenny knew Mike would be seeing his father after his operation.

If Jenny was honest, she wanted to spend just a little more time alone. And anyway, it would be good for Mike and Katie to talk – Mike had been trying to find a way to explain John's illness to his daughter and this would be a good opportunity.

They ate breakfast and chatted about names for the puppies and the new school term that was about to start in a few days. Katie managed to slip half a piece of buttered toast to Treacle and the other half to Honey. Barney stayed in the conservatory.

'Right then – ready for that walk Katie?' Mike asked, reaching for the Labrador's leads.

'Yes, let's go', Katie said eagerly, as she reached for her coat.

The dogs bounded through the hallway followed by Katie and Mike.

'Have a good time. I'll look after the pups', Jenny said.

'Bye Mum', Katie said as they disappeared through the front door.

Jenny cleared up the breakfast dishes and checked on the puppies. They were all settled and dosing on top of one another – a tangle of golden and black bodies. Jenny smiled. They were adorable.

She went into the conservatory to resume her cuddle with Barney. Just ten more minutes, she thought, wanting to make the most of the quiet time she had while the others were out. Barney had barely moved since she left him. He lay on his side, his four legs stiffly overhanging the edge of the sofa. He looked peaceful, Jenny thought.

But as she got closer to him, she noticed he was twitching. She slowly stroked his head and along his back and side.

She could feel an irregular jumping in his muscles.

He was staring blankly into space, his eyes half closed.

Then suddenly, his whole body began convulsing violently. His eyes rolled back and he began frothing and salivating from his mouth.

Jenny felt blind panic coursing through her body. 'Oh God, Barney – no. What's happening!'

As Barney jerked uncontrollably, his legs began to paddle as if he were trotting. He was shuddering and jumping as his whole body went into a full-scale seizure.

Jenny felt her stomach cramp into a tight ball of panic as she tried frantically to sooth the Doberman. She could see his tongue was hanging limply from his mouth but his legs and body were convulsing wildly. She tried to remember what to do when a patient suffered a fit. She quickly made a mental checklist. Barney was already lying on his side and there was no danger to him. He wasn't about to choke...

All she could do was wait out the fit and get him to the vet.

She needed Mike there. There was a chance they were still close to the cottage. She called out to him several times but there was no response.

Moments seemed like hours as the Doberman continued to shudder and jerk on the sofa. Jenny crouched beside him and tried to quell her rising fear as she spoke to him as soothingly as she could muster. She firmly stroked his head and side, longing for the seizure to stop.

'It's OK Barney, you'll be OK', she said to him over and over. Tears were streaming down her face as she tried to comfort her stricken companion.

'Barney; be alright. Please, please be alright', she was saying as the convulsions continued unrelentingly. Jenny felt desperate. There was nothing she could do but wait for the fit to run its course.

Gradually, the convulsions became less severe and Barney slowly stopped shuddering. The violent spasms were fading into faint muscle twitches. Jenny continued to stroke him. 'It's alright now, Barney, its stopping. You'll be alright', she said, her voice shaking with emotion as she fought to stay calm.

Barney finally lay motionless on the sofa...

Jenny froze as she waited intently for Barney to breathe. Her hand was monitoring his ribcage, willing him to take a breath.

The dog remained limp and unresponsive, his eyes glazed and unseeing.

'Barney!' Jenny shouted, 'Barney, wake up!'

There was no response. She desperately tried to deny the horrifying realisation she felt...

Jenny shook the Doberman, desperate to get him to breathe. She put her ear to his chest to listen for a heartbeat.

She could hear nothing. Barney's heart had stopped beating.
Jenny shook him again, desperate to stimulate him back to life.

She began pounding on his chest. She had to bring him back. She had to...

'Come on Barney', she shouted, a torrent of tears now streaming down her face.

Jenny screamed. 'No. Barney. Don't leave me. Come back to me'. She was beside herself with desperation.

She felt her hands trembling as she tried frantically to revive her beloved Doberman. She was shouting to him, begging him to live.

Then she felt Mike behind her, pulling her off.

She stood watching in horror for long seconds as Barney lay there; Mike trying to work out what had happened.

'He had a seizure', Jenny managed to blurt out.

Mike examined the dog carefully as Jenny urged him frantically to do something to save Barney.

Katie came running in and stopped dead in her tracks near the doorway. She was speechless and clearly shocked as she took in the harrowing scene before her.

Mike stood; his face solemn. 'He's gone, Jenny. There's nothing we can do'.

He grabbed her but she tried to pull away to save her beloved Barney. 'No. He can't be. Please – we have to do something', Jenny wailed.

Mike held her firmly by her shoulders. He looked squarely at her, his green eyes dark and solemn. 'Jenny – he's gone'.

Jenny was reeling. She could barely take it in, yet she knew in her heart her husband was right.

She'd tried to deny it but she'd felt Barney's precious soul slip away from her and all she had left now was his empty, lifeless body.

Jenny slumped to the floor next to her friend. She scooped him into her arms and held him more tightly that she'd ever done before.

How could she ever let him go!

She buried her face in his soft silky coat, her body wracked with uncontrollable sobs of grief.

Her precious Barney was gone and there was nothing she could do...

Chapter eighteen: a bargain with God

Wheelan was trying to make sense of what had happened to him. He had nobody to talk to, nobody to care about him the way Mary had. He knew he only had a matter of months to put his affairs in order before the inevitable final curtain of death closed on his life.

He had nobody to leave his belongings to, and what would happen to the manse and the chapel? He was glad he'd bought the place but what use was it to him now? He didn't have to worry about security in his retirement because there wasn't going to be a retirement. He would be dead soon. Wheelan was finding it hard to come to terms with the idea that his life was ending.

And what would become of his secrets: the drugs, the bodies hidden on the property? Wheelan knew he had things to do. He had to get rid of the evidence. But he was too sick to be dragging bodies around – it had been hard enough the first time but now he'd never cope. And what would he do with them anyway? He put the thought out of his mind for the time being. Perhaps his secrets would remain hidden and anyway, what did it matter? In a few months, he'd be gone and the constant threat of being found out would no longer exist.

He wondered if there was any point in doing anything. There was no time to achieve anything worthwhile. He'd wasted many years of his life and now it was too late to start having ambitions.

At least he could dispose of the drugs he had stashed. There wasn't much left now anyway. Perhaps he could just sell them off. He didn't want to spend the last precious months of his life dealing with scumbags anyway. A few phone calls would take care of that and he'd squander the money – on what he wasn't sure but he'd think of something.

The pain was easing thanks to the morphine and he took a swig from the bottle whenever it got too much. He was frightened – not knowing how painful it would be to die. He'd killed others but had never really considered how it might feel to go through the process of death.

He was about to find out...

He knew he wanted to die at home. The experience of being in hospital was utterly alien to him and at the very least he wanted to be somewhere familiar. Somewhere he felt secure.

He would probably die alone. He didn't want to be with strangers during his last hours and minutes on Earth. Wheelan wondered who would find him dead. Would he lie rotting for weeks until someone realised he was missing – left to decompose like the people he'd killed and dumped without so much as a prayer?

Wheelan knew praying was useless. He'd lost his faith a long time ago and he struggled to believe in an afterlife or a merciful God. Yet now he was frightened. What lay beyond death? If there was a heaven and a hell, what lay in store for him? Had his life as a minister helped him, even though he had been a total hypocrite? He had done some good hadn't he? He wasn't sure...

Wheelan reasoned that the balance was tipped toward his going to hell; if hell existed. He'd been an egotistical and cruel man with little thought for others. How would any God welcome him into Heaven? How could he repent for murdering innocent people? How could he reconcile the fact that he'd killed two people he supposedly cared about? He'd been besotted with Helen all those years ago and despite his denials, he had cared about Mary. Even the scum bag drug addict was a human being – did he really deserve to die?

Wheelan felt the emptiness in his soul. He was desperate to find God again before he died.

The alternative didn't bear thinking about...

Chapter nineteen: goodbye

Jenny had been inconsolable. She couldn't imagine life without Barney. She ached for the friend she'd known for so long. She could barely make sense of what had happened. Mike had taken charge and made her and Katie go into the kitchen while he took Barney's body out into the garden. He would have to be buried.

Katie had been too shocked even to cry. She had never witnessed a death. It had been harrowing for the little girl to witness her pet die and to see her mother so distressed.

Jenny had held her and tried to soothe her but Katie had withdrawn into herself. She was numb with shock and grief. Now Katie was sitting with the puppies in the kitchen, preferring the easy company of animals.

Jenny tried to pull herself together to comfort her daughter. Her eyes were red and swollen from crying and her mind was numb with the pain of her utter heartache. She knew she had to get through the wrenching task of burying Barney and saying goodbye to her beloved friend.

Jenny knew Katie loved Barney just as much as she did. It would be heartrending but she had to be strong for her daughter now.

'Katie, sweetheart, we'll all miss Barney. He was so special wasn't he?' Jenny said gently, trying once more to get her daughter to open up.

Finally, Katie looked up at her mother. 'Is Barney in Heaven Mum?' Her eyes were deep pools of sadness.

'Oh yes, baby, he is. He's happy and peaceful now, I promise you he is'. Jenny felt a wave of relief as she connected again with her precious daughter. She held her arms out.

Katie ran over to her mother and fell into her embrace. The two of them sobbed together for long minutes.

Jenny knew she had to tell Katie about her near death experience. It was the only thing that would reassure her daughter that Barney's soul would live on and that he was in a good place.

Jenny took a deep breath, not really knowing what to say but believing the time was right to share her experience with her little girl. 'Katie, I know for sure that Barney is going to be alright because I went to Heaven too - just for a little while. It was a wonderful place'.

Katie looked up at her mother with wonder. 'You've been to Heaven?'

'Yes, I have. A few years before you were born, I fell and injured my head. I nearly died. I felt myself leave my body and went up into a beautiful light. It was a glorious place full of love and peace and there were beautiful fields with a wide river running through it and lots of animals. Mollie, my cat from when I was little was there and she was very happy. Barney will be happy too'. Jenny said. She felt her own sadness lift as she remembered her experience, certain that Barney would be in that magical place.

'How come you didn't die like Barney?' Katie asked.

Jenny smiled. 'Your lovely Dad saved my life. And I'm very glad he did, otherwise we wouldn't have had you'. Jenny said stroking Katie's hair.

Katie looked with amazement at her mother. 'Were there people there too?' She asked.

'Yes there were. They were people I knew and loved and they were surrounded by beautiful light – in fact they *were* light. They talked to me and I know they will look after Barney'. Jenny was glad she was sharing this with her daughter. Finally Katie was seeing hope.

Katie took a moment to take it all in. 'I expect I was in Heaven too'. Katie said in her childlike innocence.

Jenny looked at her daughter. She was stunned as the inevitable realisation hit her…

In a blinding flash of inspiration, she remembered the light being that had communicated with her during her near death experience. It was Kate – the entity that had been her baby in her previous life as Helen. She appeared as a young girl but Jenny knew her soul had evolved over many lifetimes. They had shared lives over generations in various different relationships.

Katie looked into her mother's eyes. Could Katie be the reincarnation of her baby, Kate? It sounded so far-fetched, Jenny knew she would never voice her thoughts but it did make sense to her on a deep spiritual level. She remembered how the light being that was Kate had spoken to her and told her she must return. Jenny had wanted desperately to stay but Kate had told her they would share other lifetimes again.

Perhaps it was true. Kate had returned as her beautiful little Katie to re-live the life that had been stolen from them. Why had they been separated? What had happened to Helen and Kate in their previous life? Frustratingly, Jenny couldn't remember…

Katie smiled. It was almost as if she was aware of Jenny's thoughts.

'It's our secret, OK?' Jenny said, aware that Mike would probably think she was insane.

Katie nodded. 'Yes, our secret', she said. She hugged Jenny tightly, snuggling into her mother's comforting presence.

Jenny felt a deep connection with her daughter that transcended their physical, Earthly life. She felt sure that their consciousness had evolved together through eternity and that their love knew no bounds. 'Thank you Barney', Jenny sent a silent message. It was as if Barney had given them both the gift of an enlightenment that would heal their grief.

They sat entwined in each other's arms in a timeless embrace. Jenny savoured the feeling of oneness she experienced with her daughter and with the universe. For a fleeting moment, she felt the unconditional love of the pure consciousness she knew existed beyond our corporeal life.

Then the spell was broken. The puppies stirred as Mike came in from the garden. 'Are you two alright? He asked.

Jenny looked up at her husband and nodded. 'We're OK, aren't we Katie?'

Katie sat up and wiped the tears from her eyes. 'Barney's in Heaven, Dad', she said decisively.

Mike went to them and stroked his daughter's hair. 'Yes he is, sweetheart. I'm sure he'll be OK', he said. 'We should bury Barney soon. Where shall we put him?'

Jenny turned to Katie, sensing a newfound strength in them both to face the heart-wrenching task. 'What about on the cliff top, Katie? He loved it there'.

Katie nodded her agreement. The experience had been overwhelming but Jenny felt she'd helped her daughter by sharing her near death experience.

They followed Mike outside and Jenny and Katie clung to one another as Mike dug Barney's grave on the cliff top. It was a fine vantage point with views across the sea and along the coast on either side.

'Barney loved it here', Jenny said. 'It's a good place to lay him to rest'.

Mike lowered Barney's lifeless body gently into the grave. He'd hidden his body, wrapping him in his favourite blanket for Katie's sake. 'There you go old boy; rest in peace'.

Jenny felt the tears spill from her eyes once again as she contemplated life without Barney. She knew he would be at peace and that his soul would live on but she would miss his presence; his company. 'Goodbye my special friend; rest in peace. We all love you'. Jenny's voice faltered as tears spilled once more from her eyes.

Tears were streaming down Katie's face too. She was overcome with emotion as she parted with her beloved pet. 'Bye Barney. We'll miss you', she managed to say through her sobs.

Mike covered Barney's body with soil and placed several large rocks on top of the grave as a makeshift headstone. 'We'll get a proper headstone made with his name and you can put a message on it', he said to Katie.

Mike, Jenny and Katie clung together for several minutes, as they remembered Barney and said their silent goodbyes. Mike kissed them both and left them at Barney's grave while he went inside to wash the soil from his hands.

'Mum', Katie said tentatively. 'I think the Reverend might have killed Barney'. She bowed her head, regretting she hadn't told her mother before now.

'What do you mean, sweetie?' Jenny asked, puzzled.

'He kicked him in the head the other day before he collapsed on the doorstep. He hit me too but he didn't mean to do that'. Katie was such a forgiving little girl.

'Are you alright? Did he hurt you?' Jenny said, suddenly enraged.

'He didn't hurt me but I think he hurt Barney,' Katie said, now watching for her mother's reaction.

'Is that why you were so upset the other day, wanting to get Barney to the vet?' Jenny asked. Katie's behaviour was making sense at last.

Katie nodded.

'It's all right, you did exactly the right thing', Jenny's mind was racing. If Wheelan had kicked Barney's head, the injury could well have triggered a massive seizure. Her beloved Barney was dead because of that bloody deranged monster.

She was trembling with rage…

Katie was looking decidedly uncomfortable. Jenny knew it wouldn't be right to make Katie feel any worse than she did already. She must have been too worried and afraid to say anything. Jenny hugged her tightly. 'It's OK, Katie. You're a good girl and I'm so proud of you. I'm sure it was Barney's time to go to Heaven. He was an old dog', she said. She hoped she sounded convincing as she fought to hold back her furious rage at Wheelan.

They went back into the house. Mike had just finished making a phone call and was making tea. Katie made a beeline for the puppies once more but she seemed relieved that her mother hadn't been cross with her. Jenny was glad Katie had the comfort of the other dogs. It might ease the grief of Barney's death.

'Sad day', Mike said.

'Yes. I still can't believe he's gone'. Jenny was reeling with the revelation that Wheelan was responsible for Barney's death. She would tell Mike, but for now she was too incensed and irate. She would wait until Katie wasn't around. There was no point in upsetting her further today.

Mike handed Jenny a mug of tea and they wandered into the conservatory. The view was as breath taking as ever but now the scene was forever changed as Barney's grave stood to the far right on the cliff top. He would always stay in their hearts. He'd been a big part of the family. Jenny was trembling with anger. If it hadn't been for Wheelan, Barney might still be there with them instead of lying in that cold grave.

'I didn't get time to explain to Katie about Dad', Mike said. 'I heard you scream and we just ran back to the cottage'.

'I'm glad you did,' Jenny said.

'I couldn't say in front of Katie but I just called the hospital and Dad's out of surgery. The op went well and they think they've got it all'. Mike was visibly relieved.

Jenny smiled. At least something was working out well, she thought.

'We'll have to go and visit him when he's back on the ward'. Jenny was happy that the future looked positive for John.

Mike walked over to the cabinet in the conservatory and brought out a small package. He placed it in Jenny's bag. 'Now Dad's OK, we can get rid of the capataxel. Perhaps you can give it to one of your patients at the hospice and we can finally be rid of Isobel'. Mike said smiling.

Jenny thanked him. 'I'm sure I can put it to good use'. She said.

Jenny sipped her tea as her gaze ran along the coast to the manse. She thought of Wheelan and the darkness she'd sensed in his soul.

He was responsible for Barney's death.

Her utter rage slowly began to morph into an intoxicating craving for revenge…

Chapter twenty: retribution

Wheelan sat in his armchair contemplating his inevitable death. What would become of him? He felt a rising panic as he envisaged what lay beyond death. Had his malevolence earned him a place in some terrifying underworld? He was a murderer and a cruel tormentor. That much was certain. How could he go anywhere but to the very bowels of hell?

He hadn't foreseen the cancer that would steal his life. He thought he would have time to make his peace with God. But he wasn't even sure if God existed. He was frightened and alone – perhaps he should have stayed in the hospital and accepted the offer of help and counselling. He hated turning to strangers but he had to face it – he was utterly alone.

Wheelan craved his whiskey and the alcoholic stupor that would afford him a measure of escape from this horrendous reality. But just the smell of it made him feel sick. Even the familiar comfort of alcohol had turned on him. Would he be forced to face his death cold stone sober? Wheelan sipped his morphine, another addictive substance he knew he would come to rely on until the end.

What would death be like? Would he expire in agony? Would he be forced to endure a dark and terrifying loneliness through all eternity? Would he burn agonisingly slowly in hades as punishment for the suffering he'd caused in the world? Would he ever be able to redeem himself? Wheelan's head was reeling with unanswerable questions and fears...

He urgently had to find God again and make his peace...

Did he really have a soul distinct from his physical body? Would his death be the end of his conscious awareness? Would the lights go out in perpetual sleep when he died?

Wheelan felt abject fear and panic rising with every troubled thought. His mind was swimming with unwanted images of suffering and damnation.

More than anything, he wanted Mary to be there to soothe him and care for him. He glanced out into the hall. He could see her in his mind's eye as she lay at the bottom of the stairs, beseeching him to help her. He could have saved her life, yet he had been too self-absorbed in his own pathetic concerns to even notice her grief or her life ebbing away before him. She had loved him, yet he had callously rejected her and believed that this was his punishment.

Wheelan was edgy and uncomfortable. His escalating feelings of fear were becoming overwhelming. He had to find a way to come to terms with his inevitable death. He had to find the Almighty and beg for forgiveness before it was too late…

Wheelan stood awkwardly from his armchair. He was stooped with pain from his wound but he needed to escape from the haunting vision of Mary in the hallway reminding him of all he had lost. He had to get to the chapel. Perhaps he would find peace there.

Perhaps he would find God…

He clutched nervously at his wound as if it would split open as he shuffled slowly toward the door. His father's clock stood resolutely silent but Wheelan felt the intimidating echo of disapproval it appeared to be emanating.

He was lumbering along like a crippled old man. Mary's wailing and sobbing adding to the ghostly sounds that reverberated relentlessly in his head. He passed the kitchen that used to be a hubbub of activity and Mary's homely comforts. Now it lay desolate and empty; a stark reminder of what lay ahead.

Now Wheelan's beloved home had become a prison; bleak and claustrophobic. A consequence of his own wretchedness. His past deeds were closing in on him one by one like the bars of a cage. There was no escape.

He was trapped by the depravity of his own soul…

Wheelan opened the door to the fresh sea air as it tunnelled up through the valley. The saltiness was familiar and oddly comforting. He ambled toward the chapel, gravel crunching underfoot. Each tentative step became a reminder of his life as the Reverend of this parish. Ghostly images of the people from his congregation floated through his mind; they were as ethereal as the relationships he'd had with them. He'd hidden behind a façade of deceit. Nothing in his life or in his ministry had been genuine and consequently, each one of them had disappeared.

They were searching for a truth that he couldn't deliver.

Wheelan scanned the seascape before him as he reached the chapel door. The rhythmic rising and falling of the tide and the predictable changing of the seasons seemed to be the only constant left in his life. He turned the heavy iron ring handle and pushed the door open. The stone structure of the chapel echoed his shuffling footsteps as he made his way to a seat before the alter.

Wheelan sat, allowing the atmosphere of the chapel to wash over him. Shafts of brilliant sunlight were streaming through the blue and red of the stained glass windows. The peace of the building and the dappled colours of the light soothed his very being for a precious moment. He sighed deeply.

He knew his soul was lost. He knew he had strayed far from God and he wasn't at all sure he would ever find his way back.

Did he have the strength to pay his penance? If there was an afterlife, there would be no escape...

He was certain he would be judged and found guilty. What pain and suffering would he be put through before he could atone for his sins?

Wheelan uttered a prayer in the hope that God would not forsake him.

He waited for a revelation...

But there was none forthcoming. No loving embrace from God welcoming him back into the fold, no angels singing from the heavens, no disciples waiting to carry him to his celestial home.

No sign whatsoever from the Almighty...

Here in the chapel, Wheelan felt the totality of his emptiness; the sheer torment of his isolation from God.

He was more terrified than he had ever been in his life...

He bent his head and allowed tears of frustration and hopelessness to finally overwhelm him.

But they were not tears of remorse for the lives he'd taken or the suffering he'd inflicted on Mary. Nor were they for Helen, the woman he'd murdered on the cliff top; the mother of his child and the person he'd professed to love so long ago.

Utterly selfish to the end, Wheelan was desperately bargaining with God for forgiveness and a place in heaven…

+++

Jenny had felt increasingly angry at Wheelan for taking Barney away from them. She had avoided the man but now she could think of nothing else than the need to see him and talk to him – to at least have her say. She wanted to tell him that he was responsible for Barney's death and for distressing her little girl. She would tell him to stay away from her family and that he was never to go near Katie again.

Jenny watched as Katie played with the puppies. She could see it was a distraction from the pain of missing Barney. Katie and Mike were sat on the kitchen floor next to Honey's basket; Treacle was looking on from beneath the kitchen table. Jenny was utterly devoted to her little family and she wasn't going to let Wheelan upset them again, even if he *was* terminally ill.

Jenny glanced at the clock. There was plenty of time before Mike was going to the hospital to see his father. She had to answer this call from deep inside. She couldn't rest until she'd retaliated and settled her grievance with Wheelan once and for all.

'Will you two be OK if I go out for a while? I have something I need to do'. She said.

Mike looked up at her, 'Of course sweetheart. You go, we'll be fine, won't we Katie?' Mike seemed to be happily engrossed in their game with the dogs, glad to do something to help ease his daughter's sadness.

Katie smiled at her mother and nodded. Their bond had deepened since their talk earlier and Katie was beginning to accept Barney's sudden death with her realisation that he'd gone to a good place.

Jenny fetched her coat and bag and quietly left the cottage. She glanced at Barney's grave as she turned to walk the coastal path to the slipway. It was Wheelan's fault that Barney had died and she was going to make sure she gave him a piece of her mind.

As Jenny began the walk down the slipway to the beach, she could see the chapel below and the dark figure of the Reverend as he entered through the main door. From his demeanour, he was obviously in pain. It was his own stupid fault, Jenny thought. He should have stayed in hospital to recover. The stone chapel stood solidly against the elements as a sea breeze strengthened. The place still gave her the creeps. She didn't relish the thought of speaking to Wheelan but her anger was spurring her on.

Jenny made good progress toward the chapel and she pulled her coat tight against the chill wind. She reached the door and hesitated momentarily before turning the iron ring handle and pushing it open. As the heavy wooden door closed behind her, a loud thud reverberated around the chapel.

The noise had startled Wheelan who had turned to stare at her as he sat in front of the alter. She could see he was distressed and crying.

Wheelan wiped his eyes and watched as she walked down the aisle of the chapel toward him. 'Mrs Halliday', he croaked. 'I didn't expect to see you here'.

Jenny had been angry with Wheelan but his obvious suffering had triggered an innate compassion in her.

She suddenly felt a little awkward and sorry for the man. She stood over the Reverend, waiting for him to compose himself. But now she was here, she had to see this through.

Something powerful was spurring her on...

'Mind if I sit?' Jenny asked.

Wheelan squirmed uncomfortably in his seat but indicated for her to sit. It had been a long time since he'd seen her at the chapel. What did she want? Was she there in a nursing capacity? Had she been sent from the hospital to check up on him? Wheelan waited. There was an inexplicable feeling of trepidation beginning to wash over him.

Jenny saw the anguish in Wheelan's eyes. She wanted to confront him about Barney's death but despite her resentment, she couldn't help feeling a certain benevolence toward him. He was a human being, dying of cancer after all, and was obviously distressed. Her nursing instincts cut in and her anger began to soften. 'How are you Reverend? Are you coming to terms with your diagnosis?' She couldn't help but ask.

Wheelan relaxed a little and slumped back in his seat. Perhaps it was just the hospital checking on him. 'If you must know, I'm in pain and not coping very well'. Could he see concern in her eyes? There was no way he was going back into hospital, whatever she said.

'Are you taking your morphine?' Jenny asked. Her former anger was giving way to sympathy, now he was actually sat in front of her.

Too bloody right, he thought. He'd be on the whiskey too if he could stomach it. 'Yes and it does help a little'. He wished he could tell her about the emotional anguish he was feeling but telling anyone the truth was obviously out of the question.

Jenny felt compelled to at least make an effort to support him. Her training as a nurse and her compassionate work at the hospice was deeply ingrained. 'That's good. And how are you feeling about your illness? It must be a shock to be told you have cancer'. Jenny remembered the inoperable stomach tumour and the metastases she'd seen in Wheelan's abdomen.

Wheelan longed to be able to talk to someone, to relieve his conscience of all his wrongdoings. But he held back. How could this sweet woman ever understand or excuse the dreadful things he'd done? 'It wasn't a pleasant experience', Wheelan said simply.

'Do you have any relatives or friends that can take care of you?' Jenny asked. She realised she knew virtually nothing of the man's personal life. Perhaps she'd misread him after all.

Wheelan solemnly shook his head. 'No one', was all he could manage. If only she knew...

'What about your housekeeper? Would Mary be able to help out?' Jenny remembered how kind Mary had been to Katie. Surely she would be there to support him.

Wheelan cleared his throat. He would have to lie. 'Yes I'm sure she would. She's away at the moment, I think. I haven't seen her for a few days but I'll talk to her when she's back'. Wheelan awkwardly avoided Jenny's gaze. He had to hide the fact that he knew exactly where she was and that she was never coming back.

'Do you have any family, Reverend?' Jenny asked. 'Surely there must be someone'.

Wheelan hesitated. He could see the nurse was just being kind and he badly needed company right now. His thoughts turned to Kate – the little girl he'd brought up with Mary – the child that had meant so much to him. 'I had a daughter once'. Wheelan was tired of keeping up the pretence that she was simply an abandoned baby that he'd taken in. She *was* his daughter and it felt good to finally say it.

'Really?' Jenny hadn't realised.

Wheelan smiled as he remembered his little girl and heard her laughter echoing in his mind. 'Yes, her name was Kate; like your daughter. Mary, my housekeeper helped me to bring her up.' He felt the ache of regret for Mary and the pain of missing his daughter.

Jenny was startled at the name Kate. She was intrigued, wanting to know more and somehow realising that this would be an important piece of the jigsaw. 'Well, we call our daughter Katie, not Kate, but that's an amazing coincidence. Where is she now?'

Wheelan lowered his head, remembering the tragedy all those years ago. 'Sadly, she died. It was a terrible accident. Kate was only seven when she was caught out by an exceptionally high spring tide. She drowned in the cave on the headland'. Wheelan gestured toward the east.

'I'm so sorry, I didn't realise', Jenny said. She began to feel uneasy again – Wheelan was obviously upset – but she was intrigued to know more about Kate and what had happened to her. It was as if she was searching for something significant to her understanding of her own life. Something that could explain all the unnerving visions, dreams and flashbacks she'd had for so long. Would she find it here?

Wheelan needed to talk. He'd bottled up so much anguish and now this gentle woman was prepared to listen. Perhaps she'd come into his life for a reason. Perhaps she could help him come to terms with his own wretchedness. Perhaps she could even help him find God and redemption. He looked into Jenny's kindly eyes and saw a person he could trust. He'd been wrong about her.

He shuffled in his seat, the pain from his operation a stark reminded of his illness. 'Little Kate meant the world to me', Wheelan said, the words poignant as he felt the full force of the vacuous emptiness that his life had now become.

'What about her mother?' Jenny asked.

Wheelan suddenly felt extremely uncomfortable. He absently touched the old scar on his cheek as he remembered how he'd mercilessly murdered Kate's mother, Helen.

Jenny saw Wheelan touch his scar and without warning, she suddenly experienced a blinding flash of realisation. It hit her like a lightning strike…

> *Instantly she knew that Wheelan had been part of her previous life. He had featured in her near death experience.*

She gasped as she spontaneously recalled her life review. It flashed through her mind uncontrollably; revealing facts she'd long forgotten.

> *She re-lived her interactions with Wheelan exactly as she had in the dimension beyond death, she felt frightened and angry with him. She remembered seeing the menacing threat in*

> *his grey eyes and could feel a sharp silver cross in her hand as she raked his cheek.*
>
> *She saw the red blood drip onto his clerical collar.*
>
> *She felt abject terror as she saw the evil in his black eyes. There was no escape – she was trapped in his vice-like grip.*

She turned to look at his scar as he sat beside her.

> *Once again she saw a flashback of the bloody wound she had inflicted on him as he propelled her closer to the cliff edge. She had been trying to protect herself but it had been useless.*
>
> *Then she felt the cliff top crumble beneath her feet and she was falling to her death…*
>
> *Now she knew for certain she really had been Helen in her previous life and Wheelan had murdered her! She felt every detail, every nuance.*
>
> *This was no dream, it was a terrifying memory.*

Jenny was trembling with shock at the sudden and unexpected insight…

She looked again at Wheelan. She saw the same darkness in him that Helen had seen. She felt the dreadful rawness of Helen's fear.

Wheelan sensed Jenny staring at him. She'd been asking him about Helen and she was waiting for an answer. He could see she seemed agitated but it barely registered for Wheelan. He continued to wallow in self-pity as he contemplated the worthlessness of his miserable life.

Now, with her newfound knowledge, Jenny was once more seething with the intoxicating feeling of wanting to avenge her killer. She knew the truth and she wanted this depraved monster to suffer for stealing her life. This insight explained the revulsion she felt for him. Finally she understood why she'd been compelled to come to Wales and this village.

She had been seeking revenge for Helen's murder…

Her murder!

Now her killer was sat before her and more than anything, she wanted him to die. She wanted the cancer to take his life just as he had taken hers.

Life was a privilege he didn't deserve…

Jenny fought to stay in control of her escalating emotions. She desperately wanted him to confess – to admit that he'd murdered her – but Wheelan would only open up if she remained calm. She had to get the story out of him and now was the only opportunity she was going to get.

Wheelan was fidgeting in his seat, not really wanting to talk about Helen but Jenny was insistent.

She had to know.

'What happened to Kate's mother?' Jenny asked again, her voice faltering with the searing rush of adrenaline and vengeance that was coursing through her body.

'She disappeared and we didn't see her again'. Wheelan lied, hoping that Jenny wouldn't probe any further, yet he found it strangely comforting to talk to her. Perhaps he'd feel better if he got things off his chest.

Jenny knew full well what had happened to Helen – she had actually *been* Helen! Now she wanted to know more about her past life.

The utter rage she felt about Barney's death was also returning, but she had to keep her cool.

She wondered if she could prise more information out of Wheelan about Helen's life before she got him to confess to murder. So far he hadn't even mentioned Helen's name.

'Tell me more about Kate's mother. What was her name? Where did she live?' Jenny asked.

Wheelan wondered why the nurse was so damned interested in Helen. Perhaps she was just making conversation, he thought. He supposed there was no harm in talking about the past – it might even help him to put things into perspective. 'Her name was Helen', Wheelan said simply.

There was the confirmation, Jenny thought. She knew from the depths of her soul it was all true but she wanted him to tell her more. She wanted his confession. She wanted him to know she had come back for revenge and she wanted his remorse.

Wheelan hesitated to say more. But he had already verified the facts beyond doubt for Jenny. Her feelings of trepidation about Mrs Baxter, the photograph of Helen and Terry, the flashbacks of her as Helen in that house – it was all true! Even Katie somehow knew about Helen's life at the hands of the aunt and uncle through her painting.

Now she was reeling. Jenny badly wanted to challenge Wheelan about Helen's death. She wanted to let him know she had come back from the dead to confront him and get her revenge for stealing her life. It was all utterly surreal, yet here she was exposing the evidence that Wheelan was her murderer. What would he do, she wondered? Would he believe her if she told him she was the reincarnation of Helen and that she was back for revenge?

Jenny was about to confront Wheelan but there was a further revelation to come.

She suddenly had another fleeting blaze of enlightenment...

> In a strange paradigm shift, she remembered her experience as Helen – how she'd given birth to her daughter and called her Kate. She remembered the loneliness and the wrenching decision she'd made to leave her baby at the chapel. She had to make a life for them both if she was to escape the cruelty of her aunt and uncle – the Baxters'.
>
> Jenny remembered how Helen had looked into Wheelan's menacing eyes and realised that he had raped her in that dark, filthy place.
>
> Wheelan was Kate's father.
>
> Jenny experienced the full force of the pain and anguish that Helen had felt in that moment of revelation...

Jenny looked up at the alter and saw in her mind's eye her precious baby Kate. She finally understood what had happened and was horrified at what she had done before her untimely death.

Helen had laid her baby on the alter with a note for the Reverend, not realising that he'd been the vile rapist that had attacked her.

Now she knew...

The beautiful being of light that had spoken to her during her near death experience was Kate – Helen's baby.

Wheelan's baby...

Somehow, their worlds had merged and she was finally closing in on the truth. It was more horrifying than she could ever have imagined. She wondered what other evil acts this monster had committed...

Jenny could barely contain the torrent of pent up words she had for him as she sat beside her killer.

'What about Kate?' Jenny said. She was almost afraid to know the truth about what had become of Helen's baby.

Her baby...

Yet despite her anger, Jenny knew that Kate had been taken care of. She knew Kate had been peaceful when she'd met her and communicated with her in the dimension that lay beyond death. Jenny was certain she was now back in physical form as her daughter Katie.

They were together and Wheelan couldn't harm them now...

Wheelan pictured his little girl and felt the full force of his desolation and despair. Everything that had been good in his life had disappeared and it had been his fault. Helen was gone, Mary was gone and due to his thoughtless neglect, Kate had drowned in the cave. Whatever lay beyond, Wheelan wasn't sure he wanted to live.

He wasn't sure he *deserved* to live.

Wheelan could barely answer Jenny's question as he broke down in tears. His body was wracked with sobs as he confronted his wretchedness. As a young man he'd been given the opportunity to mould his life into a force for good. He was a chapel minister with a lifetime to give to others and the opportunity to change people's lives for the better. But instead he had become a hypocrite. His life had been one big lie and he'd chosen to cultivate a violent brutality that served only his own egotistical needs. Wheelan knew he was weak and cowardly.

If God existed, how could he ever forgive him for what he had done?

Lucas Wheelan thought of his daughter Kate and finally felt remorse. Tears stung at his eyes as he felt the aching loss of his wasted life and of his daughter's life cut short. He slumped toward Jenny, clutching at her as if she had the power to take away his pain and anguish.

He gave into his tears and wailed...

Silently, he was begging for God's forgiveness.

Jenny sat firm as Wheelan leaned into her, sobbing. She badly wanted revenge, yet she also saw a frightened human being, desperate to come to terms with the cancer that would inevitably kill him. Jenny could see he was searching for forgiveness and redemption. He was a man of God that had lost his faith and lost his way; yet needed proof that his soul would be saved.

As Wheelan wept like a child on her arm, Jenny remembered her near death experience and how the being of light that was Kate had spoken to her. She understood why she'd had to return to her body and her life. She remembered what she had learned from the unconditional love that emanated from that incredible place and from the souls that inhabited it.

Jenny knew that there was no judgement. There was no right and wrong.

There was only experience…

Jenny understood that we are merely actors in a repeating cycle of life and death. Eventually, we will experience bliss in an expanded spiritual realm because of our experiences; our joy and our suffering.

Jenny remembered her profound understanding of the purpose of existence – to expand and evolve the conscious universe…

Jenny looked down at Wheelan as he sobbed, clutching at her arm. She knew that he might confess to Helen's murder. He might confess to other deeds he'd carried out in his life. She could get the confession she wanted and even the remorse she'd craved from him.

And *he* may feel better for unburdening his conscience…

Should she give him that gift?

Now she knew the truth about the past they had shared and the roles they had acted out over several lifetimes.

She knew – wasn't that enough?

Jenny also knew that Wheelan would die. He would experience the same profound and unconditional love that she had, despite his wrongdoings. She knew he would review his life and would finally understand the purpose of his actions and his misery. He would meet with light beings that loved him and they would welcome him to his temporary home before reincarnating into his next adventure into physical life. She knew he would feel the peace of that indescribably beautiful realm and realise that there was no everlasting retribution for his sins – there was no eternal hell.

Jenny felt an instinctive compassion for this tortured soul. She had been given a gift of knowledge that gave her the power to make a choice about Wheelan's future.

She could tell him about the incredible love and acceptance that awaited him. That would surely ease his pain while he was dying...

Or she could stay silent...

Jenny felt conflicted. She understood what blissful ecstasy lay beyond the veil of death, yet she couldn't help feeling the anger that still surged inside her. Wheelan had murdered her and taken her from her child in her previous life. He had also just taken Barney from her family.

Her anger was still raw...

In rare moments of enlightenment, she wanted to share the love she knew belonged to everyone, but she was still playing out her life in the here and now. She was living the reality of her physical existence and she was feeling the intensity of the pain and rage that Wheelan had instigated. Could she overcome those very real feelings?

She wasn't sure…

Wheelan's tears finally ebbed away and he sat up, drying his eyes. 'I'm sorry. It's all too much for me', he blubbered.

Jenny looked into his grey eyes. She felt a heady mixture of compassion and hatred for the man that had caused her and her loved ones so much pain and detriment. She knew there would be much more he had to atone for. Only he knew what suffering he'd caused others.

'It's OK, Reverend', Jenny said. But her feelings were in turmoil.

What should she do? How could she reconcile her compassion for this human being against her anger at him for what he had done?

Wheelan felt compelled to confess his sins. He wanted to relieve his conscience and he felt sure that Jenny would listen. He hoped she would understand. He looked into her kindly eyes and knew he had to unburden himself or he would surely go mad. 'I've done some terrible things', he said, as he was about to reveal his darkest secrets.

Jenny held up a hand warning him not to say more. 'Please', she said, 'I don't want to hear it'. Jenny knew what he was about to say but strangely the need for his confession was gone. She no longer wanted to hear the words, or his remorse. She knew in her heart what he had done and that was enough…

But she couldn't help but feel the hatred and anger toward him that she'd carried with her over two lifetimes.

He would experience the blissful revelations about death when his time came. Yet Jenny couldn't bring herself to tell him the truth about the indescribably beautiful afterlife she had discovered.

She knew he would have to live with his regrets; to face the consequences of his actions; to suffer the anguish he'd created for himself.

Yet, she felt a deep compassion for him as a human being. She too had realised the preciousness of life when she had faced death.

She knew what she must do…

Jenny reached into her bag for the capataxel that Mike had given her.

'Reverend, this medication will put your cancer into remission. It will give you a chance at a longer life'. Jenny held out the package.

Wheelan was stunned. 'What do you mean? What is it? I thought there was no cure.'

'It's an experimental drug, used as a last resort for advanced cancer. It's been shown to reduce the size of carcinogenic tumours and even miraculously cure terminal cancer like yours. You may even be considered for surgery in a few weeks'. Jenny could see the expression of complete astonishment on Wheelan's face. His eyes were still wet with tears.

She went on. 'This has to be our secret though. It's not actually available yet and it's prohibitively expensive. Let's just stick to the story that your cancer went into spontaneous remission. These things do happen – you could call it a miracle'. Jenny waited for his agreement before she let him take the capataxel from her.

Wheelan nodded. 'Of course – it will be our secret. How much does it cost? My money is all tied up in this chapel and the manse. I can't pay for it'. Wheelan suddenly regretted spending his illicit drug money.

'I don't want your money, Reverend', Jenny said. 'But perhaps you'd consider leaving your assets to the hospice as a sign of goodwill?' It would be a fitting tribute, she reasoned, and worth far more than the cost of a pack of capataxel. She hoped she could trust him…

Wheelan agreed. He was certainly relieved to be thrown this unexpected lifeline. He would have more time to come to terms with his eventual death and perhaps to find God before he was cast into the eternity of hell and damnation.

Wheelan was not looking forward to more misery, desolation and loneliness but he was far too frightened to die. He clung tightly to the small packet that would save his life.

But could he bring himself to take the medication? Did he want to prolong his wretched life? Now Mary had gone, he was alone and frightened.

Perhaps giving in to death would be preferable than to go on living the hell that he himself had created.

Wheelan felt tortured…

'Why are you doing this, Mrs Halliday?' Wheelan had to ask. He knew there must be far worthier causes than him.

'You'll work it out someday', she said. Jenny knew he would have to wait for the peace and love that she had been denied when she was forced to return to her body.

She looked into Wheelan's eyes. The menacing darkness in his soul was still there. She knew he would struggle to find peace in this lifetime.

Jenny stood to leave. She felt a pang of guilt at what she had done. Should she have relieved his suffering with the privileged knowledge she had of death?

She could have let him die so he could discover the unbelievable love and acceptance for himself instead of prolonging his miserable life.

She still wasn't sure…

'Thank you nurse', Wheelan said.

Jenny nodded. It was too late to change her mind now. She turned and strode down the aisle of the chapel toward the door, her footsteps echoing around the stone walls. She turned toward the Reverend. He looked frail and lonely. There would be a lot more pain and anguish to come as he reckoned with his life and came to terms with death.

He still had his tortured soul to contend with…

Jenny opened the chapel door and stepped outside into the sea air. As she started the climb up the slipway toward her home and her family, she finally felt free.

The circle of karma was complete.

She had her life to live with so much to look forward to and so much happiness yet to experience.

She thought of Mike and her beautiful daughter and was glad to be alive.

For news of Oliver Rixon's next book, please visit:

www.hollybluepublishing.co.uk

Connect with Oliver on Goodreads:
www.goodreads.com

Printed in Great Britain
by Amazon.co.uk, Ltd.,
Marston Gate.